For Matt

Nurse Wesley's standing in the front of the room acting like it's perfectly normal to have words like *puberty* and *hormones* and *safe sex* on the blackboard. The other guys in my class are calling out words for certain body parts—partly to see if they count and partly because Nurse Wesley's chest shakes when she writes on the board. *Nurse Breastly,* they call her. Meanwhile, I'm taking inventory of the number of hairs on the back of Paul Badowski's neck, who I purposely sat behind because he has the most enormous head in the class, and wondering if it's scientifically possible for a person to die of embarrassment.

It's Human Sexuality class, which of all the cruel and unusual things they do to kids in high school has to be the cruelest. And, according to my brother Jake, who went through this last year, the worst is yet to come, when Nurse Wesley brings in an actual real-life condom and shows us how to use it by putting it on a banana. When I heard that, I told my mother I planned to come down with the Ebola virus or diphtheria or something; but she said I was going to school whether I liked it or not, because as the single mother of three boys, she was relying on the Pittsburgh public school system to handle the sex education.

"Why can't I wait till I really need it?" I said. "Like when I'm in my forties."

She just laughed.

"But it's not age-appropriate for me," I said, which is technically true, on account of me only being thirteen from skipping a grade when I was little.

But my mom said if I was old enough to go on eBay to trade baseball cards, I was old enough to learn about human sexuality.

So, here I am, sitting behind Paul Badowski, trying to remember if sweaty palms and an elevated pulse are two of the warning signs of a heart attack, when he raises his hand.

I send urgent, heavy-duty ESP vibes to the back of his head, telling him to go back to sleep like he was in math class. But he waves his hand so hard it's like he's hanging on to the last piece of wreckage from the

Titanic, and the S.S. *Carpathia* has just sailed into view. "Oooh, oooh," he says.

Nurse Wesley looks in his direction. Which means she looks in my direction. Which means I slide so far down in my seat I look like I have a terminal case of curvature of the spine.

"Yes, Paul," she says.

"Nurse Br . . ." He starts laughing. "I mean, Nurse Wesley?"

"Yes?"

Whatever it is Badowski has to say, it's so hysterical he can't get it out.

"Paul," she says, "the class is waiting."

"Nurse Wesley . . ." He takes a deep breath. "What's a midlife crisis?"

"A midlife crisis?" You can tell she doesn't think this is especially funny. "It's really not something we usually cover in Human Sexuality class, but I suppose, if you want to know . . ." Her voice trails off.

"Is that what Toby Malone is going through?"

At the sound of my name, the entire class turns around to look at me. At which point I decide I'm glad that Nurse Wesley is a certified health-care professional, because in a minute I'm going to need CPR.

She, however, doesn't seem to see the gravity of the

situation. She makes one of those superpatient teacherly faces that you can tell means that if she weren't a teacher she'd be laughing. Which is what pretty much everyone else in the class is doing.

For some reason, they seem to think that a person who happens to be starting to get prematurely gray hair in ninth grade is the funniest thing in the world. Which, I can tell you from personal experience, it's not. If they were even halfway politically correct, they might stop and think that maybe it's a symptom of that rare disease where kids suddenly turn into old people and shrivel up and die. Which it's not, although that's what I thought until my mom finally took me to the doctor, who said it's probably just a lack of pigment or something. Still, looking like a senior citizen when you're a freshman in high school isn't exactly a laughing matter, if you know what I mean.

I pray for a fire drill or a bomb scare or an announcement over the PA system saying we can all go home for the day on account of a previously unknown multicultural holiday.

But Nurse Wesley, who's one of those teachers who honestly thinks she's supposed to answer kids' questions even if they're ridiculous, is trying to explain what a midlife crisis is. She's saying something about how when people get older they sometimes get motorcycles or sports cars to make themselves feel better, but no one's really listening. Most of them are still looking at my hair.

She tells everyone to turn around and look at her. Everyone turns around. Then she holds up a strand of her own hair, which is kind of a no-color color. "Gray hair is nothing to worry about," she says. "Right, Toby?"

At which point everyone turns back around to look at me again. I decide she's going to have to treat everybody for whiplash if she keeps this up.

I shake my head no, even though technically I *do* think it's something to worry about, although it's something I try *not* to worry about, since worrying about it probably actually gives me more gray hairs.

After that, Nurse Wesley gets back to business, but you can tell she's pretty much given up on the technical part of the program and is moving into the emotionally meaningful conclusion, where she talks about how what we're going through is a natural and beautiful part of the cycle of life, which makes her sound like a sort of modern-day school-nurse Rafiki—which of course means people stop paying attention.

Badowski gives me a no-hard-feelings-even-though-I-just-destroyed-your-self-esteem punch in the arm.

And Arthur, who's pretty much been my best friend since fourth grade, holds up a piece of paper that says HUMAN SEXUALITY SUCKS. Which means my heart rate pretty much goes back to normal and I go back to staring at the back of Badowski's neck.

Until I look across the aisle and realize that Martha MacDowell is looking at me again. Martha MacDowell's this girl who sits alphabetically in front of me in homeroom and who smells really good, like clean laundry right out of the dryer, and who has hair the color of butterscotch syrup, and who I'm pretty sure has been looking at me lately.

I go back to counting the hairs on the back of Badowski's neck while also trying to figure out if the look Martha MacDowell was giving me was the kind of pitying look you give someone who has a fatal aging disease, or the kind of kindhearted look you give someone who's just had a near-death experience.

All of which means that when class is finally over, I bolt out of there and get on my skateboard and head for Mr. D's Candy and Collectibles, where I can hang out with somebody who really *is* an actual senior citizen and find out if he got the Dave Parker rookie card he was bidding for on eBay last week.

* * *

When I get to Mr. D's—which is technically just the front room of an old house in a neighborhood near school and not in a mall like a regular store—he's standing at the door waiting for me in his Mister Rogers sweater. He holds the door open, then shuffles back inside in these prehistoric red plaid bedroom slippers he always wears; it occurs to me that in all the years I've been coming here, I've never seen Mr. D in actual shoes.

Which is actually saying something, on account of the fact that I've been coming to Mr. D's since I was a little kid, back when I used to spend my whole allowance, plus whatever change I could find between the cushions of my dad's La-Z-Boy, on baseball cards. Back then, I mostly bought whichever players my dad liked or whoever Jake told me to buy; but after my dad left and Jake got too mature to be into baseball cards, I kept at it. I moved up from buying regular cards, the ones that come with the dusty pink gum, to rare cards, like rookie cards of guys who went on to become famous, and cards of pretty much anyone who ever played for the Pirates.

Which I pay for by doing odd jobs for Mr. D—like tying up cardboard boxes for recycling, or vacuuming the rug, or watching the store while he goes to the bathroom. Which I do every Tuesday, Thursday, and Saturday. Which means I pretty much have the best collection of vintage Pirates cards of anybody I know, even though, technically, I don't know that many people who still collect baseball cards.

Mr. D tosses me a pack of WarHeads—underhand, slow-pitch style, not even looking in my direction—which is his way of saying hello and which he doesn't even charge me for.

"Did you get the Parker?" I say.

He runs his hand through his hair, which is wild and crazy like Albert Einstein's but which actually makes him look sort of punk for an old guy.

"The answer to some prayers," he says, "is waiting."

Which is the kind of wise, mysterious, Yoda-type thing Mr. D always says. Which doesn't even answer the question, if you want to get technical about it. But which is okay with me, since Mr. D gets a big kick out of trying to make me figure out what he really means.

"I'm gonna take that for a yes," I say.

"You may," he says.

"Okay if I spend some quality time with it?"

Quality time is when Mr. D lets me just sit there and admire a card I don't have the money for, which he doesn't let regular kids do, since he says they manhandle the cards and then don't even buy them.

"You may," he says. "Or . . ." He waits for a second. "You may want to do something else first." I figure this is Jedi Master talk for saying I ought to Windex the display cases before I start drooling over a card that'd probably cost me two weeks' worth of tying up the recycling. He motions to me to come over to the counter. Then he reaches underneath and pulls out a small, dented, Army-green box, which he opens with a key from a chain around his neck.

There, inside, along with some old savings bonds and a picture of his beloved dead wife, Dolores, is a mint-condition 1962 Willie Stargell rookie card.

A Stargell rookie card is something holy. Willie Stargell is the one and only guy who spent his whole career with the Pirates. Not like Barry Bonds or Bobby Bonilla or about a thousand other guys who left Pittsburgh for better money or better teams or better towns. Willie Stargell's the guy who, even though he retired before I was even born, *still* holds the team career record for home runs (475) and grand slams (11). The guy everyone called Pops, the guy who pretty much single-handedly won the '79 Series with the all-time best clutch homer in Pirates history. The guy my dad said was the heart and soul of the team before the Pirates, and pretty much the whole town of Pittsburgh, went downhill. The guy whose card I've been dreaming of ever since I started collecting. Mr. D hands it to me.

I'm afraid to even breathe on it. Then I realize I'm not actually breathing.

"Whadya think?" Mr. D says.

"I think I'm having a stroke."

"What?"

Telling a guy Mr. D's age that you're having a stroke is probably not too cool. "Where'd you find it?" I say.

"On the Internet," he says. "From a guy in Cincinnati."

All I can do is nod my head up and down like one of those bobble-head toys they give away at McDonald's.

"So . . ." Mr. D says. "How does it feel?"

"Amazing," I say.

Amazing. And awful. Amazing because it actually exists, because a mint Stargell rookie card was sitting under the counter in Mr. D's shop that very afternoon while I was in Human Sexuality class watching a video called "Our Changing Bodies."

And awful because I'm pretty much the biggest

Stargell fan in the entire universe—even though technically I probably inherited the job from my dad—and
there's no way I can buy it. I hand it back to Mr. D
before my palms get sweaty and disintegrate it.

"What're you doing?"

"You better put it back in the strongbox," I say. "In
case a freak tornado or a forest fire comes along."

Mr. D ignores this advice.

"Toby," he says. "What you wish for, you will come
to believe in."

I don't get it.

"It's yours," he says.

"You're giving it to me?"

He nods.

"For free?" I say. If I have to break down cardboard
boxes in exchange for a '62 Stargell, I'll be working at
Mr. D's till I really *am* a senior citizen.

He laughs. "Yes," he says. "I'm giving it to you."

And all of a sudden it's like one of those TV talk
show moments when people hug and cry and get all
emotionally out of control. Mr. D pats his back pants
pocket, which means he's fishing around for the blue
plaid handkerchief that's always sticking out of it. I've
only ever seen him use it once, when we were talking
about his beloved dead wife, Dolores, after which he

turned his back toward me and blew his nose with a big honk, after which both of us didn't exactly know what to do.

Meanwhile, I'm feeling like a little kid who finally actually gets a pony for Christmas after waiting for 185 years, which in the movies pretty much only happens when the kid has cancer, or when some formerly mean adult finally sees the error of their ways. Which makes the fact that I'm suddenly the owner of a mint condition Stargell rookie card even more amazing since it's *not* because of cancer or anything bad, but just because Mr. D—who doesn't have that much money and isn't even related to me—for no reason at all just gave me the one thing I wanted more than anything in the world.

I know I should do something. Or say something. Something serious but not cheesy, something like Thank you except way better than that. The kind of thing my dad would know to do.

Like the manly man's no-shake handshake, which my dad gave me the day he moved out. He was already done packing stuff like socks and shaving cream and his clock radio, but I was still dragging a Hefty bag around the house filling it up with things. Stuff like his oldies record collection and a picture of me when I had no front teeth and his Pirates beer mug, and pretty much anything I could think of to keep the actual moment of him walking out the door from happening. Until finally he made me stop.

He took my hand, which looked puny and babyish next to his, and closed his hand around mine. His hand felt as big as a polar bear paw. Then he covered my hand with both of his and just held it there, not shaking it or anything. And I knew then that we both knew what was happening, but that we were going to get through it without getting all emotionally out of control.

I peek out from under the brim of my baseball cap and see Mr. D fumbling around for the handkerchief. I stick out my hand. He puts his hand out. His hand is nothing like my dad's. It's lightweight and bony and his skin is soft and smooth, like an old, polished stone. I put my other hand on top of his and just hold it, not shaking it or anything. And I know then that we both know what's happening, but that we're going to get through it without getting all emotionally out of control.

Then he thumps me on the back, surprisingly hard for a guy who was wheezing a couple minutes ago, and says I shouldn't be hanging around with an old guy like him. "You should be out with the other young Turks," he says, which isn't like an ethnic group or anything; it's an old-time expression meaning a person's friends.

So I say okay. Because now that Mr. D and I have narrowly escaped having to get all emotionally out of control, all I want to do is jump on my skateboard and go out and show the whole world the Stargell.

Well, not technically the whole world. Just my dad. I can just picture him, shaking his head and saying Holy mackerel, which is about the worst language he ever uses. He won't believe it. He'll clap me on the back and say how Stargell's the boss, and how not many kids would realize what it means to have a Stargell rookie card, and how I'm a chip off the old block being a die-hard Stargell man. It'll definitely blow him away.

When he sees it.

When he comes back home and I can show it to him.

In the meantime, though, there's Jake. Jake, the formerly undisputed king of baseball trivia. Jake, who practically had a complete set of the '92 Eastern Division Championship team until he turned mature and quit collecting. Jake, who last year pretty much single-handedly won the division play-offs with a sixth-inning grand slam that even got written up in the actual newspaper—not just the school paper—and got compared to Stargell's '79 pennant winner. Jake, who even though he's too cool now to personally want a Stargell rookie card, will understand how amazing my having one is.

I can just picture him. He'll whoop and yelp and holler and call me The Man. Or he'll give me the high-five—low-five—wrist-clench secret handshake from back in our Little League days. Or he'll smack me in the back of the head in a way that you can tell means he's psyched for me. Then he'll yell out to our mom, who doesn't know anything about sports, and our eight-year-old brother, Eli—who wears a cowboy hat and calls his bike Tonto and who also could care less about sports—and they'll get psyched about it. Just because Jake's psyched about it.

Except that when I get home, Jake just sits on the couch staring at whatever's for sale on the Home Shopping Network.

Not only is he not in a yelping-hollering-goofing-around kind of mood, which, to tell you the truth, he's actually never in anymore, he's in one of those moods when he's there but not really *there*. When he's stoned.

Which makes me want to headlock him and wrestle him and maybe even actually sort of hurt him so that he comes back to being his normal self. Or else sneak out of the house before he sees me seeing him that way and maybe come back later when he's his normal self.

Instead, I stand between him and the TV.

"You'll never guess what I have," I say, all out of breath.

He doesn't say anything.

"C'mon," I say. "Try to guess."

He doesn't try to guess. He just keeps staring at the TV. His eyes are red and itchy-looking.

"You'll never guess," I say.

He finally looks at me, except that it's like he's sort of looking past me. "If I'll never guess," he says, "why don't you just tell me?"

I don't exactly know how to respond to that logic, so I set the card down on the rug in front of him.

He doesn't do anything. He doesn't whoop or holler or even move a muscle.

"What did it cost you?" he says finally.

I happen to know that it's technically worth more than two years' of my allowance. But I don't tell him that. I also don't tell him that Mr. D *gave* it to me, which is a highly private fact that you don't tell somebody, especially somebody who doesn't whoop or holler or thump you on the back when you show him a mint condition Stargell rookie card and who only wants to know what it cost.

I shrug.

He gives me an annoyed look; then he sort of smiles, and I can see the pointy teeth on the side of his mouth—like when our former dog Harriet the Horrible got old and unpredictable and started snapping at little kids in the neighborhood and we had to put her to sleep—and I wonder if he's going to start laughing like crazy the way he does when he's like this or if he's just going to completely forget that I'm even here.

So I pick up the Stargell and leave.

I cross the front yard where Eli is sitting on Tonto with the kickstand down. He's wearing his cowboy hat and yelling at Tonto to giddyup, even though technically he's not even moving. He's only allowed to ride on the sidewalk and there are no sidewalks here in Colonial Mews, this cheesy, fake-historic apartment complex where we moved after our dad left.

I grab my skateboard and head out across the yard.

As soon as Eli sees me, he tells Tonto to whoa. "Where you going?" he says.

I look across the parking lot, over toward the highway. Everything good—our old house, Mr. D's, the park—is on the other side of the highway, which according to our mom is a death trap.

I shrug. "Nowhere."

"Can I come?"

"Mom says you're not allowed."

"Please?"

I don't know what to say. I feel bad for Eli not being able to actually ride his bike anywhere like a normal kid. But the good thing about Eli is that he isn't a normal kid; he's the kind of kid who, if you tell him he can't do something normal, does something weird, like pretending his bike is a horse right out in the front yard, and isn't even embarrassed about it.

"It's okay," he says after a minute. "Tonto's pretty tired from the cattle drive, aren't you, boy?"

Tonto doesn't let on if he's tired or not, so I just get on my skateboard and ride across the parking lot, and out to the overpass. I don't go back to the old neighborhood, though. I just stand up on the overpass and watch the cars whoosh by on the highway underneath until it's practically dinnertime.

Dinner that night is shrimp cocktail, courtesy of the Food King. The Food King is this giant frozen-food warehouse across from the mall. The Food King is also a person: he's one of our mom's clients at the Hairport, a rich guy who owns the Food King, but who always gives her a box of frozen food when she cuts his hair instead of giving her an actual tip. He even stars in his own highly lame TV commercials, which feature him personally, wearing a crown and a fur-trimmed cape. Our mom says he likes it when the other stylists at the Hairport call him Your Highness.

Jake calls him Your Heinie.

"Looks like dinner came from Your Heinie tonight," says Jake. His voice has a slow-motion sound, but no one notices except me.

Eli, who's in second grade and who, therefore, thinks any mention of body parts is insanely funny, practically has a spaz attack trying not to laugh. "The food came from your heinie," he says, crinkling up his nose, which has about 185 million freckles on it, and pointing to his butt, which isn't much of a butt on account of him being so skinny. "Get it?"

Our mom gives him a look like she has some kind of major, long-term headache. Which is pretty much how she's looked ever since our dad left, which some-times makes me think that maybe she might really be sick, maybe even dying of some rare incurable disease without knowing it. The only time she doesn't look like maybe she's secretly, fatally ill is when Jake makes her laugh.

"Methinks His Heinie is wooing our fair mother," Jake says.

Our mom pretends to be annoyed, but you can tell she's not.

"Perhaps he wants to make her his Food Queen, courting her with shrimp and wiener."

At the mention of the word wiener, Eli's eyes bug out from under his cowboy hat, and he grabs his side like he's just been shot in the ribs or something. Then he falls off his chair. "Wiener!" he shrieks from the floor, where he's writhing around like crazy. "Jake said 'wiener'!"

The aforementioned wiener is a cocktail wiener. Technically, 144 cocktail wieners. That's the other problem with the Food King. His food comes in bulk, usually a gross of some kind of party food—12 dozen stuffed mushroom caps, 12 dozen crab cakes, or 12 dozen mini-pizzas—appetizers we turn into dinners by eating lots and lots of them.

"Ask His Heinie if he'll give us ice-cream sand-wiches next time," Jake says.

"Yeah," says Eli. "Ice-cream sandwiches from his heinie, get it?"

At which point our mom morphs back into her terminal illness self. "Enough," she says, dead serious. "Enough of this heinie talk."

Eli climbs back into his chair, and we all lower our eyes and pick at our shrimp cocktail. A split second later, Eli and Jake burst out laughing.

"What?" she says. "What's so funny?"

Eli falls on the floor again. "You said . . ." He can't get the words out. He squirms around like he's dying. Jake acts innocent.

My mom looks to me to explain.

"You said 'heinie,'" I say. "It sounds funny when you say it."

She smiles. Then her shoulders shake. Then she starts laughing. She's one of those people who laugh until they cry, who quiets down then gets started up all over again. She's also the kind of person who looks pretty when she laughs, pretty in a Mom kind of way, pretty and maybe not secretly on the verge of death after all.

* * *

After dinner my mom's putting the dishes in the dishwasher, Eli's out in the front with Tonto, and I'm sitting on the couch watching the Pirates suck. It's the bottom of the eighth, the Pirates are down by two, and Pokey Reese is on deck when Jake comes in.

"Hey look, Toby." He points at the TV, which is showing a commercial where an old guy in a tie and a short-sleeved business shirt is combing Just for Men through his hair. "You should ask Mom to buy some of that stuff for you."

I don't tell Jake that I already secretly bought some Just for Men at the drugstore a couple of weeks ago, which meant I couldn't bid on a '75 Matty Alou on eBay. And that it didn't do anything except make my gray hairs look sort of orangish, until the next time I washed my hair, and it all came out in the shower. Instead, I throw a pillow at Jake, which misses him because he ducks just in time and it hits a lamp. Mom comes in and tells us to go outside and find a more appropriate way to burn off our testosterone.

I'm still zipping my sweatshirt up by the time Jake's out the door. I yell at him to wait up.

"Hey," says Eli as he sees Jake crossing the front yard. "Where are you guys going?"

Jake cocks his head toward the highway.

"Can I come?" says Eli.

Jake puts his hand on Eli's shoulder. "They don't allow horses over there," he says.

"It's okay," says Eli, stroking Tonto's mane. "We have work to do around the ranch."

Jake pats Eli on the head and takes off. I yell at him to wait up again. He looks over his shoulder at me, but he doesn't slow down. He doesn't speed up, either, so I run till I catch up with him.

"Whadya wanna do?" I say.

He's got his headphones on, so I tap him on the shoulder. I look at him from the side and decide that my mom is right, that Jake does look like Josh Hartnett. He's got shaggy brown hair that always looks perfectly messed up, crinkly eyes that practically disappear when he laughs, and a potential future manly man's jawline. He doesn't notice me tapping him on the shoulder, so I lift one headphone away from his ear.

"Whadya wanna do?" This time I say it loud enough so he can hear me through the music.

"What?" he says.

Obviously, it wasn't loud enough. "Wanna play Werewolf?" I'm practically shouting.

Werewolf is this game Jake invented back when we

lived in the old house. The kid who's the werewolf chases all the other kids around in the dark until everybody is either home-free behind the McMullens' garage or captured by the werewolf. Jake was always the werewolf on account of him being an expert at coming up with ways to ambush people, like jumping down out of the Nevilles' peach tree or off the roof of the McMullens' toolshed. And I was pretty much always the last one to get caught, on account of me being an expert watcher. Even in the dark, I knew, from the clinking of the chain, when someone bumped into the Dawsons' swing set or from the shushing of branches, when someone was cutting through Mrs. Dunaway's bushes on their way to make a break for home.

Jake and I, we were untouchable at Werewolf—until our dad left, and we moved, and Jake got all cool and uninterested in things he considered immature, which is pretty much everything we did at the old house.

"Werewolf," I say. "One on one."

I wait for him to mock me. Or squeeze my neck till I cry uncle. Or maybe even just completely ignore me. But he actually says okay. Which makes me think that maybe, at least for the time being, he's the old Jake after all.

We decide that home base is the bench in ye olde

village green, which is actually just this plot of crab-grass in the middle of Colonial Mews. Then Jake, who's automatically the werewolf without us even discussing it, counts to 100 while I hide.

There aren't nearly as many good hiding places at Colonial Mews as there were at the old house, but I find ways to keep on the move, crouching behind bushes and dodging behind parked cars, ducking under streetlights and creeping through the little AstroTurf backyards some people have here. After about ten minutes or so I decide that I've gotten better than ever at Werewolf.

But after about fifteen minutes I decide that maybe Jake's gotten bored and walked over to the mall.

Which makes me go from feeling like the James Bond of Colonial Mews, to feeling like some kind of overgrown psycho-toddler loser. The only way to know for sure is to make a break for ye olde village green.

I peek out from the laundry room doorway where I'm hiding, sprint across the grass, then slip behind the Dumpster, Mission Impossible style. Then I twist the toe of my sneaker into the grass—better traction, like Jake taught me—ready to put on the final burst of speed toward ye olde bench when I feel this incredible whack between my shoulder blades.

The air flies out of my lungs in a whoosh, and the next thing I know Jake's on top of me, and I'm on the ground with my face in the dirt and my legs churning up the grass like one of those jackrabbits on the Nature Channel whose legs keep running even though he's already being eaten by a cheetah.

Jake pins me within a matter of seconds.

"Give in, Dillweed?"

Dillweed is Jake's favorite insult for me. Back in her cooking days, our mom had a spice called dillweed which Jake said was named after me. I pretend that I hated being called Dillweed, but to tell you the truth, I actually sort of liked it since he never calls anyone else Dillweed and since he never calls me Dillweed in front of anyone else.

"Nope." I grit my teeth. "Never!"

Jake shoves my head under his armpit. But I break free, roll over, and get in position to use the Crazy Leg, this wrestling move when you straddle the person and squeeze his legs between your knees.

Jake begs for mercy. I tighten my grip. He promises to take out the garbage when it's my night. He promises to let me borrow his Discman. But I tighten up even more until he's squirming and yelping, squirming and laughing, ripping handfuls of grass out of the ground and throwing them in the air at me.

I let up a minute, just to show a little mercy, since this is a historic event, this being the first time on record that I've ever pinned him. "How'd you catch me?" I say. "Where were you hiding?"

Jake cocks his elbow to point toward the Dumpster.

"You jumped off the Dumpster?"

Jake smiles; the Dumpster move is one of his best ever.

It's right about then that we notice Andy Timmons standing there watching us. Andy Timmons—this kid who has an actual goatee and who hangs out in the parking lot before school smoking cigarettes and drinking coffee, and who everyone knows is a drug dealer—is standing in ye olde village green, holding a bottle of some kind of whisky. "How cute," he says. "A little brotherly love."

Jake pushes me off him and gets up. Then he puts his arm around Andy Timmons's shoulders and starts walking away.

I jump up and trot along after them. I remind myself of Harriet the Horrible, who even when you were done playing with her kept trying to give you her slobbery ball, but I don't know exactly what else to do.

I run ahead and grab the hose next to the Dumpster.

"Wanna drink?" I say. To Jake, not Andy Timmons.

Jake doesn't answer. He takes the bottle from Andy Timmons and drinks it down almost to the bottom. Then he grabs the hose and wets down his hair. He swings his head back and his hair sticks up like a rock star.

"Now whadya wanna do?" I say.

Jake looks sideways at Andy Timmons. Whatever it is he's going to do, it doesn't include me. He drops the hose and walks to the curb with Andy Timmons.

I pick up the hose and wrap it up, making perfect circles one inside the other, like I'm a soldier wrapping up the American flag, all serious, like the future of democracy depends on it. Jake turns back toward me.

"Toby," he yells over to me. "Tell Mom I'm going over to the park to shoot hoops."

He's lying. I can tell because he's being way too casual, like the time he convinced me to trade him my Cal Ripken for a Ricky Henderson. I also know he's lying since whenever he tells my mom he's "shooting hoops," he comes in after she's asleep and eats pretty much everything in the pantry, which I know from the videos Mr. Fontaine, the guidance counselor, shows during Freedom from Chemical Dependency Week, is one of the things people do when they're high. What I don't know is what you're supposed to do when it's your brother and not somebody in a video. What I do is clean everything up afterward so our mom doesn't find out.

"So, you'll tell her?" he says.

I go back to the job of wrapping up the hose.

Jake hands the bottle back to Andy Timmons, then walks toward me. Andy Timmons comes along.

"You were tough tonight, Toby," Jake says, socking me on the shoulder. "You really got me with the Crazy Leg."

I go from frowning like a U. S. Marine to grinning like ye olde village idiot.

A car horn honks from somewhere down the street. Andy Timmons asks Jake if he's coming or not.

Jake grabs hold of my arm. "You'll tell her?"

The horn honks again.

Jake punches me again, hard this time. I jab him back, but my fist just plows through the air, because by then he's already gone.

When I get back home, my mom's sitting at the table with our cat, Mr. Furry, curled up in the chair behind her. Mr. Furry's technically a girl, although we didn't know that back when we first got her. She's also technically everyone's cat, even though the only person she actually ever hangs out with is Eli, and who, if you ask me, is pretty lame and stuck-up as a pet. Especially compared to Harriet the Horrible, who at least was always glad to see you and who thumped her tail on you when she sat next to you on the couch, and who was a great pet, even if she did have bad breath.

My mom's back is toward me, but I can see she's paying the bills, because the checkbook is in front of her with the numbers crossed out, scribbled over, and crossed out again. She moves one bill from the have-to-pay to the have-to-wait pile, sniffs, and blows her nose into a paper towel. Mr. Furry jumps off the chair and leaves, her tail in the air.

I picture myself going in and putting my arm around my mom. Or at least getting her a tissue instead of a paper towel. Or maybe making her a baloney-and-mustard sandwich. Or just acting like everything's okay, which maybe it would be if we just acted like it was. But instead I back out of the room.

I also stop by the front door and check for a letter from my dad or a postcard like the one he sent us from California that had a picture of something called the Lonesome Pine—a supposedly famous tree on a beach in California, but without any *Baywatch*-type surfers or anything—and a message on the back saying how we'll all be living out in sunny California as soon as he finds a job. He FedExed us a bunch of amazing presents the first Christmas, but no letters and no money since then. Ever since we moved, and my mom sold most of his stuff at a yard sale, there's sort of an unspoken rule: we don't speak about him.

Sometimes I pretend he's on a long business trip, like the executive dads on TV. Sometimes I wonder if maybe he's in a coma on account of being in an accident on the California freeway and no one knows about him having a family back in Pittsburgh. But mostly I worry that when he comes back, I might not recognize him.

Which is why I saved the picture of all of us at the Implosion. In the picture, we're all sitting on the grass in the park where we used to watch the fireworks. Our mom, who back then looked more like someone's big sister than someone's mom, is smiling, and our dad, who looks like Bruce Springsteen, except with less hair, is holding a beer and looking out of the picture frame at something far away. Jake and I have on our Little League shirts, and Eli's hiding under his yellow baby blankie.

In the picture, we're sitting in the park along with pretty much the whole town, looking across the river at the mill where my dad and his buddies used to work, waiting for it to get blown up. Imploded, actually. Which meant that they put dynamite in strategic locations so that the whole thing would collapse in on itself. It was like some weird, science-fiction block party. Old steelworkers and their wives were sitting on picnic blankets listening to polka music, college kids were waving protest banners, and little kids were goofing around on the swing set. When they should've been acting serious and respectful like we were at a funeral, which technically we were.

Out of nowhere, the crowd started counting down like it was New Year's Eve.

"Three! Two! One!"

Eli yelled, "Blast off!" A bunch of people shouted, "Implosion!"

What came next was nothing. People started fidgeting. Someone in the crowd behind us booed.

Then there was a white flash at the base of the plant. People oohed. There was another spark a little way from the first one. People aahhed. Then, finally, there was a chain reaction of sparks all around the base. There was no noise really, just a flimsy sounding *pop* a few seconds after each spark. All of a sudden, the whole building began to fold in on itself, section by section, one after the other. Then there was a groan, a sound I felt—actually felt—in a spot in the middle of my chest. A minute later, the two giant smokestacks in the middle of the plant crumpled and sank to the ground, while a bunch of birds erupted from the stacks and flew off.

After that the steel company was supposed to build a new mill on the same spot, but they didn't. Which meant my dad got laid off, after which the unemployment ran out, and he had to take a job driving a giant trash–vacuum cleaner truck around the mall at night and drinking beer with his friends during the day. Until finally one day about a year ago he left for California.

My mom stayed in bed for a week straight, crying and smoking cigarettes and not answering the phone and not making us go to school. Which was fun at first since she stayed up in her room sleeping or watching Lifetime TV, and we got to watch the Cartoon Network and eat Pringles and Pop Tarts and pretty much whatever we wanted. But which got to be sort of scary after a while, when she wouldn't get up even though there was nothing left to eat but peanut butter straight from the jar. Until finally one day, out of nowhere, she got out of bed and suddenly turned really busy, hauling all my dad's stuff out onto the front lawn for a yard sale and then selling the house and getting a job at the Hairport, after which she's pretty much looked like she has a terminal headache ever since.

My mom tried to sell the Implosion picture at the yard sale, saying the frame was at least worth something. But I grabbed it off a card table where our entire life was being pawed through by people who asked if you'd take a quarter for something that's worth a million dollars if it's yours. I brought it to ye olde condo where I set it up in the den.

My mom keeps turning it facedown when she cleans. I keep putting it back up.

I turn the picture faceup, then I shuffle through the mail, even though I can tell from the feel of it that there's no letter from him. Nothing personal, just a catalog, which is technically for my mom but which Jake steals so he can look at the pages with women in their underwear, and an American Express bill. I lift the rubber band from around the bundle and pry the credit card bill free, secret-agent style. Then I stand there wondering exactly what it is I was planning to do with it. Eat it?

I slip the envelope into my back pocket and go upstairs, where I lock the bathroom door and count my gray hairs. I quit after I get to thirty-two. Then I sit on the fluffy green thing that covers the toilet seat and wonder if pulling out the eleven hairs I found a couple weeks ago caused twice as many more to grow back like my mom said it would. Then I get up and try 185 different ways of combing my hair so I won't look like a thirteen-year-old senior citizen, until I finally give up and put my baseball cap on.

Which reminds me that I need to get my mom to sign a permission slip for tryouts stating that if I get brain damage on account of getting hit in the head with a line drive, or getting struck by lightning in the outfield and I'm paralyzed for life and have to wear diapers and eat through a straw, that she won't sue the school. Although it doesn't technically mention lightning and diapers, it does say that parents agree to buy their kids cleats and to pay for the uniforms to be dry-cleaned at the end of the year.

I decide that's not something you can ask a mother to think about when she's blowing her nose on a paper towel because she can't pay the bills and when she has one son who's out with a known drug dealer and another son who doesn't have the guts to come in and make her a baloney-and-mustard sandwich, and when she herself may be suffering from a rare terminal disease.

So I sign it myself and go up to my room and stare at the Stargell.

Which I've done about 185 thousand times since I got it. Which is probably roughly equal to once every seventeen seconds. Which you would think would get boring but it gets more amazing the more I do it. Even if during the other seventeen seconds when I'm not looking at it, I'm *thinking* about looking at it. And even if when I'm not looking at it or planning on looking at it, I'm thinking about how much my dad's gonna love looking at it.

At 1:16 in the morning, I'm still staring at the Stargell. Technically, I'm arranging Bill Matlock and Tim Foli and Phil Garner and the rest of the '79 World Series team on the same page in my binder and trying to stay awake, when the front door creaks opens.

Which probably in a normal house is just a normal sound, but which in our house is like a car alarm going *whoop, whoop, whoop* right inside the front door.

I jump out of bed and run downstairs.

Jake's standing there watching the coat rack, which he just banged into, wobble back and forth. His eyes are squinty and his mouth is hanging open. "Check it out, man," he says.

"Shut up," I say. "You'll wake Mom."

He gives me the look. It's the same look my dad used to give me at 1:16 or 2:55 or 3:39 in the morning.

The look that, in my dad's case, meant he was going to get all emotional and recite the list of people he loved—like the guys at the mill or his old high school baseball coach or Lucky, the famous dog from his childhood who was supposedly so smart she did everything on his paper route except collect the money.

Or he'd give me the look that meant that he was going to get all bummed out and recite the other list, the people who he said "just didn't get it"—like the Republicans or the management at the mill or the guy at the unemployment office who gave him the same load of crap he gave him the week before. Then he'd just shake his head like *he* was the one who just didn't get it, which was actually worse than watching him get all choked up about some long-lost dog from his childhood.

Either look meant I had about ten seconds to get

Dad inside and get him up the steps before he woke my mom up. Which I was usually able to do, especially if I stayed up reading *The Ultimate Baseball Encyclopedia* until he came in. But when I wasn't, it meant that my mom came down to breakfast the next day with her eyes all puffy from crying and my dad had to sleep on the La-Z-Boy that night and they went back to fighting and Eli went back to sucking his thumb from under his blankie and Jake and I had to be on our good behavior until they made up. But after a while they stopped making up, which meant my mom's eyes were puffy pretty much all the time and my dad slept on the La-Z-Boy pretty much all the time until he left.

The look, in Jake's case, means his eyes are like mirrors. I can't tell what he's thinking. All I can see is my own scared self looking back at me.

I grab the coat rack and steady it. Then I grab Jake by the shoulders and steer him in the direction of the stairs. He misses the first step and starts laughing.

"Shhh." I clap one hand over his mouth and squeeze him by the back of the neck with the other, then I push him up the steps, nudging my knee into his back, step by step, until we finally get to our room.

I get him into our room, where he kicks off his jeans and starts to climb up to his bunk on the top. He wobbles a little, sort of like the coat rack, then bolts into the bathroom and throws up. I swing the door closed, flick on the fan, and pray our mom hasn't heard anything.

While Jake is hanging his head over the toilet, I get out the can of Citrus Magic, this orangey-smelling spray that says it makes odors disappear magically. Our mom opens the door and walks in, wearing her pink robe with the coffee stain down the front.

"Honey?" she says to Jake. "Are you sick?"

She sniffs and I give the room another blast of Citrus Magic.

Jake doesn't look up. "Food poisoning," he says, wiping his mouth with the back of his hand. "The shrimp cocktail."

She looks confused. "That's funny. No one else got sick. . . ." Her face gets that long-term fatal headache look.

"Me, too," I say all of a sudden. "I don't feel too good, either."

"Did you throw up?"

I shrug. "Not exactly, but my stomach feels weird. I couldn't sleep." Both of which are technically true.

She pats the pockets of her robe like she's looking for cigarettes, even though she just quit smoking again last week, and you know it's one of those times that she wishes she wasn't someone's mother, that she could have a smoke and go back to bed and not have to worry about things like barfed-up shrimp cocktail.

I tell her to go back to bed, and that if we're old enough to handle Human Sexuality class, we're old enough to take care of this. Which we do, mostly by Jake going to bed and me fumigating the entire place with Citrus Magic.

The next morning on the way to the bus stop I ask Jake about how he managed to get up on the Dumpster the night before.

"My manly upper-body strength," he says.

Then I try to think of a way to ask him about him and Andy Timmons without acting like I care.

"Last night," I say.

Jake won't look at me straight on.

"It wasn't the shrimp cocktail," I say.

Jake doesn't let on if he hears or not. He's eyeing my new baseball cap. "Gimme that for a second," he says. "I'll fix it for you."

I hand it over sort of cautiously. Jake puts it on his own head, cups his hand around the brim, and squeezes it. He takes it off, examines it, then curls the brim a little more till it has the rounded, broken-in shape he considers cool. He puts it on my head, snugs it down, and steps back to admire his work.

"There," he says, tugging it down till it practically covers my eyes. "Now you won't look like such a dork."

And instead of being mad at him like I planned on, I'm actually sort of grateful to him for at least doing a big brotherly kind of thing.

Which confuses me more than trying to walk to the bus stop with my hat pulled down so far I can hardly see where I'm going.

Which means I'm a couple steps behind Jake when a white car pulls up with Andy Timmons and his goatee in the driver's seat. I peek out from under the brim of my hat and watch as Jake gets in and leaves me standing there on the sidewalk looking like a dork after all.

That day at the end of lunch—after everybody except the janitor and a couple of chess geeks have left the cafeteria—I pull the American Express bill out of my back pocket and throw it into a trash can, where it lands on top of somebody's leftover meat loaf. Where hopefully it'll get mixed in with all the crusts from kids' peanut butter sandwiches and the fruit that mothers always pack but which nobody ever eats and all the pencil shavings and old test papers from the school, and get carted away to the dump, where it'll get buried underneath a bunch of flat tires and broken toilet seats. Which won't solve the problem of my mom having an American Express bill that is never going to make it out of the have-to-wait pile, but which at least is something.

As soon as the bell rings, I head down the hall to meet Arthur at his locker so we can walk to tryouts together. Before I even get there, I can see him because of his flaming red hair. Even though it's probably the worst possible hair a person can have—except for prematurely gray hair—he seems to like what he calls his "defining feature," which sounds like something his mom made up to make him feel better about it.

He's standing in front of his locker with all his books and papers and old sweatshirts and sneakers and candy bar wrappers dumped out on the floor.

"I can't find my permission slip," he says.

I feel for mine in my back pocket.

"You get yours signed?" he says.

"Yup," I say, which isn't technically a lie. It's signed. By me.

I lift up one of his old sweatshirts, which I'm

pretty sure he's been dragging around from one locker to another since fourth grade, and hunt for the permission slip. Arthur asks if I want anything to eat. His dad has an office job and his mom is a nurse, so he always has money for after-school junk food.

"Whadya have today?" I say.

"What do I have?" He gives me a maniac grin. "Gonorrhea."

Arthur has pretty much the same sense of humor as Eli. He thinks any sentences containing words for private bodily parts or private bodily functions or words not generally used outside the confines of Human Sexuality class are hysterical. Lately, he's especially fond of otherwise normal words such as *but* and *screw* and *nut*. All of which is highly embarrassing for me, especially the gonorrhea line, which is a reference to the fact that up until Human Sexuality class I thought gonorrhea was an intestinal problem, like diarrhea, something I was stupid enough to share with Arthur.

What he actually has is a Butterfinger, a Snickers, a pack of Little Debbies, and some Rolos. I'm pretty hungry, having not eaten the beef goulash on account of it maybe having Mad Cow disease; so I go for the Little Debbies.

"You got your new stuff?" he says, pawing through

a bunch of crumpled-up papers. "It says on the form that we have to buy our own cleats."

I don't say anything; I hold his biology book up and shake out all the papers inside.

"I got new cleats last night," he says. "And a Barry Bonds batting glove."

Arthur's always getting new stuff. He has Nintendo, Game Cube, *and* PS2.

"And a . . . you know." He points to his crotch.

I don't get it.

"A *nut* cup." He says this in a fake whisper which is actually pretty loud and which is obviously heard by a bunch of girls walking by, including Martha MacDowell, who up until Arthur mentioned the aforementioned nut cup was looking at me in a way that wasn't kindhearted or pitying but which was completely normal.

I smack Arthur on the back of the head and give Martha MacDowell a look that I hope is also completely normal and go back to looking for his permission slip. She and the other girls go past and Arthur finds his permission slip inside the pocket of his official Pirates backpack which reminds me that I haven't told Arthur yet about the Stargell.

"Hey," I say. "You'll never believe what I got."

I don't wait for him to answer because I know he'll say gonorrhea or scabies or one of the other disgusting diseases we learned about last week. "A Stargell rookie card."

I watch his face for a minute, waiting for this piece of information to sink in. "A mint condition '62."

Even Arthur, who's the kind of Pirates fan who likes to own all the stuff with the logo on it but doesn't actually know a whole lot about the good old days, knows about Stargell.

"No way."

"Way."

For once, he doesn't know what to say. His mouth actually hangs open. The next thing I know he's picking me up, physically picking me up, like ball players do to their coaches when they win a big game, and he's trying to carry me around the hallway.

Which, even though it's highly embarrassing, is the kind of thing I like about Arthur. He's the kind of kid who, even though he's got Nintendo and Game Cube and PS2 and new cleats and a new glove and a new nut cup and pretty much whatever he wants without even having to spend his allowance, actually gets really happy when somebody else gets what they want. He's also the kind of person who's really out there with his feelings. Which my mom says is because he's a redhead and redheads are often pretty out-there people emotionally.

Which, even I have to admit, can actually be sort of good, at least on certain occasions. Like when a person finally gets something they've been wanting their whole life.

When we get to the locker room, Arthur shows me the aforementioned nut cup, which, in my opinion, is way too personal to even talk about let alone be seen in public with. Which means Arthur thinks it's funny to throw it at me. Which means I actually have to physically touch it to throw it back at him, which grosses me out enough that I overthrow the stupid thing. Which lands at Coach Gillis's feet.

"Malone?" he says. "Does this belong to you?" He holds the nut cup in the air so that everyone in a 185-mile radius can see it.

I decide I will definitely not live long enough to even get *through* puberty if this kind of stress keeps up.

The coach throws me the nut cup, which I drop, probably ruining my chances of making catcher before even getting out of the locker room.

I pick it up, trying not to fully touch it.

Coach Gillis looks at me like he's waiting for something.

"Thank you," I say even though I'm not feeling especially thankful for being handed a nut cup that isn't even mine.

He's still looking at me. "Malone?" he says. "Where's your brother?"

"I dunno," I say. I pretty much figured Jake was somewhere else in the locker room, like in the VIP section with other guys from last year's team, and that he wouldn't necessarily want me coming up and being associated with him.

Coach Gillis shakes his head like he's disgusted, which he probably is from having to deal with things like nut cups. Then he sticks his thumbs inside the waistband of his pants, hitches them up, and walks away.

Arthur and Badowski and I are crossing the parking lot on the way to the practice field when we see the girls' team up ahead also crossing the parking lot. At which point I notice a girl with a butterscotch-colored ponytail sticking out of a baseball cap.

"Hey, look," says Arthur. "It's Martha MacDowell."

I try to look without looking like I'm looking.

"She's hot," says Badowski. Saying someone is hot is something guys in our class say all the time about certain girls; for some reason, though, when Badowski says it about Martha MacDowell, it sort of annoys me.

I accidentally on purpose trip him.

He looks offended.

"That's for saying I'm having a midlife crisis in Human Sexuality class," I say.

We walk the rest of the way to the field with the two of them talking about tryouts and me wondering what's going on with me that I'm all of a sudden noticing things like girls' ponytails and caring about people calling other people hot.

The new-kid-baseball-player-wannabes, like me and Arthur and Badowski, are drilling grounders in a patch of grass that's about as far as you can get from the field without being in the bleachers, while the kids from last year's team are playing a scrimmage. No one's watching us, not even the assistant-assistant coach, who's a student teacher and who wandered away from our drill after five minutes to watch the real players. *We're* not even watching ourselves, on account of trying to also watch the real players, too.

Who are pretty much the guys from last year's team. All except for Jake, who, even though I figure he's pretty much guaranteed to make the team on account of being the MVP from last year, should've been here for tryouts. I try not to think about this, though, since every time I do, I screw up, which just makes me think about it more.

The scrimmage is in the bottom of the third when the catcher, who I remember making an amazing rip-off-the-face-mask foul-ball grab in the top of the fourth at Division Championships last year, jumps up from behind the plate and charges down the line to tag a runner heading toward home. Except that he falls facedown in the dust halfway between home and third. He grabs the back of his leg and makes an injured face.

Coach Gillis comes over and is concerned for about a half a minute, then he starts yelling at the kid for not stretching like he told him to. The assistant coach helps the kid up, and the assistant-assistant student-teacher coach trots over with an ice bag. The kid hobbles off the field and Coach Gillis starts shouting for somebody named Truman.

Badowski yells out "Coach! Coach!" which means that for once, everybody—the coach, the assistant coach, the assistant-assistant coach, and even the real players—are looking over at us.

"Truman moved to Florida," Badowski says.

"Florida?" yells Coach Gillis. "What the hell did he move to Florida for?"

"His dad got a job down there," says Badowski.

"What am I supposed to do for a backup catcher?"

Badowski shrugs.

The coach looks around the field. Then he calls out my name.

At that point I just about have an advance attack of post-traumatic stress syndrome.

I point to myself in the chest. "Me?"

"You catch, right?"

I nod yes, because I do catch. Then I shake no, because if he's asking if I catch right the answer is technically no, since I catch left.

"Do you want to catch?" Coach Gillis says. "Yes or no?"

I just stand there.

Arthur shoves me in the back. "He wants to," he yells. "He played catcher in middle school. And Little League. He definitely wants to."

That's the world's biggest understatement. Being catcher, aside from it having the absolute coolest equipment of any position, is the best spot on the team. The catcher is the one and only guy who—

because he's the one and only guy facing out while the whole rest of the team is facing in—can see the whole game happening right in front of him. The pitcher can't see anything going on behind him and the guys on the bases and in the outfield can't see what the pitcher's doing. Only the catcher can see the whole thing. Which means that being catcher is like being a fan with the best seat in the house while also actually being on the team.

I look over and see the kid who was catcher last year unbuckling his shin guards. Arthur shoves me again, and the next thing I know, I'm walking the 185 miles between where we were drilling and where the real players were playing, trying to decide if I should put the shin guards and the chest pad on right away and not hold things up any more or if I should stretch like the other kid got yelled at for not doing.

Then Coach Gillis announces that everybody should take a water break, which gives me time to stretch. I try to do it in a way that's obvious enough for him to notice, but subtle enough not to make everybody think I'm sucking up. Then I put on the gear, snap down the face mask, and catch.

Which I don't suck at.

I don't do anything amazing. But I also don't do

any of the hundreds of stupid, bonehead, bush-league, game-losing things I could have done. I just catch.

And then practice is over and everyone's back in the locker room and Arthur makes like he's going to pick me up for the second time that day—but he doesn't. Maybe because even he realizes it's one thing to pick up your friend when no one's looking, and when you're celebrating a once-in-a-lifetime event. And it's another thing entirely to pick up a kid in a locker room full of older guys when all you're celebrating is one kid getting a pulled hamstring and another kid moving to Florida and me at least not sucking on the first day of tryouts.

Instead, he pulls my socks down, which looks like he's busting on me, but is his way of saying congratulations on not sucking. And I snap the waistband of his pants, which looks like I'm busting on him, but is me trying to at least say thanks for helping make it happen.

On the way home, I stop by Mr. D's. He's online chatting with some guy in Harrisburg who has a Jason Kendall for sale. He tosses me a pack of WarHeads without even looking up.

When he signs off I ask if the guy sold it to him.

He gives me a Yoda look. "Happiness," he says,

running his hand through his Einstein hair, "is having what you want and wanting what you have."

I don't come right out and say it, but I'm pretty sure that means the guy wanted more than Mr. D could afford. I hope that's not because he spent all his money on the Stargell.

"Here to spend some quality time with the Parker?" he asks.

I shake my head. I'm here to tell him that I might not be able to come in on Tuesdays and Thursdays on account of maybe, possibly, hopefully making the team.

Me not coming in probably isn't an actual problem, since hardly any real customers ever come in except me, but which still makes me worry about how Mr. D's gonna manage tying up the recycling on his own or reaching the top shelf where the baseball trivia books are, just in the event that some know-it-all kid *does* come in.

He looks at me, then over at my backpack which I dumped by the door when I came in and which has my baseball glove hanging off the strap.

"Tryouts start today?" he says.

I just look at him and wonder how he always knows stuff without me actually telling him.

"Pretty quick for an old guy, don't you think?"

"Yeah," I say. "No. I mean, you're not that old."

He just smiles.

"It probably won't happen," I say. "But if I do, you know, make the team, I might not be able to come in so much."

"Oh," he says. "That's okay."

"Like maybe not on school days," I say. "But I can still definitely come on Saturdays, and do the recycling. No matter what."

Mr. D says okay again.

"Just save all the recycling for then," I say. "I can do it all on Saturdays, okay?"

Mr. D puts his hand on my shoulder. "Toby," he says. "I believe you," he says. "Like I believe in electricity."

I don't get it.

He turns the light switch on, then off. "I believe in it even if I don't see it," he says.

This is one of those wise, mysterious Yoda-type moments when whatever Mr. D says makes total sense and which I decide to use next time I need something profound and meaningful to put in a book report or something. Although as soon as I'm not with him, I don't exactly understand it anymore. Which, I guess, is why it's a wise, mysterious Yoda-type thing.

My mom's car isn't in the space out in front of our apartment when I get home from Mr. D's; instead there's a beat-up white car with a Grateful Dead sticker on the bumper. As soon as I open the door I can see Jake in the den watching TV with Andy Timmons and his goatee, along with some other kid I've never seen before. Andy Timmons is sprawled out on the couch and his boots are propped up on our mom's glass coffee table. The stereo and the TV are both on and bags of chips and Doritos and Cheetos and bottles of Yoohoo and Mountain Dew are lying all over the place.

I stand in the doorway watching them watching TV and waiting for them to move. They don't. Which reminds me of the time Jake and I spied on a guard at a wax museum, waiting for him to do something like blink his eyes or scratch his butt so we'd be able to tell if he was real or if he was part of the museum. After a while, when all they do is sit there like wax museum people, I go up to my room, which is also Jake's and Eli's room, and close the door.

At which point, I turn into psycho ADD house-wife—stacking up old copies of *Mad* magazine in chronological order, matching up all the tube socks on the floor, and sorting Eli's Beanie Babies by species.

Then, as soon as I clear a place on the rug, I lie down and listen through the floor to what's going on downstairs. Which sucks because the rug is scratchy and it smells like gym clothes somebody left in their locker over the weekend and because listening to people who are downstairs eating Cheetos when your stomach upstairs is growling for them makes you even more hungry.

With all the noise from the TV and the stereo, I can only pick up sound effects, not actual words. One of the people downstairs suggests something; I can tell because the other voices go up like they're agreeing. Someone walks into the kitchen. It gets quiet, then they laugh. I can't hear what happens next but whatever it is cracks them up even more. Jake's laughing his insane laugh, the one that used to make me practically wet my pants when I was little.

After a while I wonder why I'm upstairs lying on a scratchy rug that smells like the boys' locker room when I could be downstairs laughing at whatever Jake's laughing at and eating Cheetos and drinking Mountain Dew. So I get up, kick a few old *Mad* magazines into the spot where I was lying, and go downstairs.

When I walk in, Jake's grabbing his stomach and laughing without making any noise and Andy Timmons is pointing at the kid I'd never seen before and snickering. The kid, who's wearing a T-shirt that says "Pissing Off the Whole World, One Person at a Time," has a red dot in the middle of his forehead and another one in his hair, which you can tell from the look on his face, he knows nothing about. He reminds me of Maurice, this kid down the block who goes to school on one of those little half-buses and who my mom says we aren't allowed to call retarded.

"What?" the kid says. "What's so funny?"

The red dots are left over from the yard sale. The Pissing-Off-the-World kid spins around, like Harriet the Horrible used to do when she was chasing her tail, and I notice that there's a red dot on the butt of his saggy jeans, too. I make a sort of half-laugh/half-cough sound so they know I'm there. Jake looks up.

"Hey, man," he says. "You're home."

He doesn't sound exactly glad I'm home—which I always am at this time of day—but he doesn't sound exactly not glad either, so I go in. I sit on the arm of one of the chairs since all the other seats are taken and Mr. Furry is sitting in my usual spot on the couch.

"I don't get it," says the kid with the red dots, looking over his shoulder at me. "What?"

While Jake and Andy Timmons are looking at the Pissing-Off-the-World Kid, I dig my hand into the bag of Cheetos. There's nothing in it except some former Cheeto dust at the bottom. I reach for the bag of chips, which is also empty, then half-laugh/half-cough again to cover up for my stomach growling.

Jake gets up and puts his arm around the kid with the red dots. "Vince, my man," he says, secretly sticking another dot on his shoulder. "You need to chill."

"What?" the kid named Vince says again. "I still don't get it."

Jake and Andy Timmons laugh like this is the funniest thing they've ever seen. It is sort of comical, but not exactly funny, if you ask me, like the way it's sort of entertaining to watch Maurice playing make-believe games in his front yard all by himself, but which is also sort of weird, too.

I try to act like it's no big deal, like your brother getting high in your house with a future hardened criminal and a kid who looks like he's retarded when your terminally stressed-out and possibly fatally ill mom and your completely innocent cowboy-hat-wearing little brother are about to walk in the door any minute is completely normal, and not something that makes you feel like a car alarm is going off inside your head.

I get up, crumple up the Cheeto bag, grab a couple empty cans of Mountain Dew, and head for the trash can in the kitchen, where I hope to get some kind of bright idea that will shut off the car-alarm feeling.

The sound of fake audience applause comes from the TV, then Jake laughs his insane laugh. I step to the doorway of the den to see what's going on. The red dots are everywhere now. On the couch, the TV, the La-Z-Boy, the coffee table, the lamp, the rug, the magazines. The room is like one big yard sale. And Andy Timmons is standing right in the middle of everything, the package of red dots in one hand, a pen in the other, putting a price tag on our mom's spider plant. Jake's slapping his hand on his thigh, the way people do on TV when something's funny. Vince's mouth is hanging open, a red dot on the nose of his glasses.

The next thing I know, Andy Timmons is coming toward me, holding out a red dot, which would mean I was for sale like the rest of the furniture.

Except that Andy Timmons walks right past me and toward the Implosion family picture I saved from the real yard sale. He peels a red dot off the pad and goes to put it on the frame.

"Our mother won't like that," I say. I sound like a total dweeb loser, like the crabby little kid in *The Cat in the Hat* who freaks out when Thing One and Thing Two fly kites in the house and who keeps saying, "Our mother won't like this. Not one little bit." I clear my throat.

"That frame's worth something," I say, like that's a better explanation.

Jake looks at me like I'm a lower life-form. "You need to chill," he says.

Which is the same thing he said to Vince a minute ago, in a way that you could tell he really liked Vince, even though Vince was acting like one of the kids on Maurice's bus. But which, when he says it to me, you can tell he is embarrassed of me, even though I'm only acting like myself.

"Mom'll be home any minute," I say.

Jake gives me a disgusted look. "God, Toby," he says. "You are such a dillweed."

As soon as they leave, I turn into turbo-drive psycho ADD housewife. I get a new trash bag from under the kitchen sink, dump all the soda cans and ashes and everything else, tie it up, and carry it outside. Just to be safe, I take it across the parking lot and throw it in the Dumpster.

Then I peel the stickers off the furniture so they won't be there when our mom gets home, which makes me think of the mother in *The Cat in the Hat* again. You never actually see her. You just see the bow on the tip of her high-heeled shoe when she comes home after the mess is all cleaned up. "Did you children have fun?" she says. "Tell me. What did you do?"

The cranky little kid just sits there. "Should we tell her about it?" he says. "Now what should we do?" Then he looks right at you while you're reading the book. "What would *you* do if your mother asked *you*?"

That night my mom's giggling on the telephone. Which is weird because she doesn't laugh that much anymore, especially when the phone rings. She says it's usually someone trying to get her to buy something or somebody trying to get her to pay for something she already bought. It's also weird because it isn't her normal Mom laugh. It's more like the way girls in my class put their hands over their mouths and giggle when certain guys walk by in the lunchroom. Jake's one of those guys.

"I just can't," she says. "There's no one to watch the boys." She twirls the phone cord around her fingers, then twirls herself around the cord. "Okay, okay," she says. "I guess so. Just for a little while. "She giggles again, then says good-bye and I go back to pretending to read the sports section.

She sort of half-walks/half-runs through the room,

then disappears upstairs, humming. After a while I follow her upstairs to find out what's going on.

By the time I get there, she's in her room with the door shut. Jake and Eli are in our room playing Nintendo. I pull my baseball card binder down from the shelf and sit down at the desk and look at the Stargell for the zillionth time.

There's only one word that comes close to describing the way the Stargell makes me feel. Rich. Not rich like the Food King or like Arthur, but like I have something that makes me special.

After a while, our mom peeks in. Her hair is in some kind of weird upswept style like a bride's and she's wearing a clingy red top, a black skirt, and high heels.

"Does this make me look fat?" she says, checking herself out in the mirror.

To tell you the truth, the red top is sticking to her chest in a way that makes me feel shy just looking at her. But at least she doesn't look like maybe she's secretly dying of an incurable disease. "No," I say. "You look good, Mom."

She smoothes her skirt across her hips, then shrugs. "Jake," she says. "Put that thing on pause for a minute."

Jake and Eli keep playing, so she has to step over all

the *Mad* magazines and tube socks and Beanie Babies which are all over the place again, and stand in front of the Nintendo, blocking their view. Eli groans. Jake elbows him to shut up.

"Now," she says. "You boys listen to Jake. Do whatever he tells you. I'll be back soon. Okay?"

Jake whistles. "You look foxy, Ma," he says.

"You think so?"

I wonder what's different about him telling her she looks good and me telling her, but decide not to say anything.

She kisses us each good-bye, smelling all flowery and hopeful and leaving lipstick gunk on my cheek which I wait to wipe off till she's gone, and then I go back to staring at the Stargell and feeling rich.

After a while, Jake sets the controller on the rug, stands up, and leans over me.

"How come you're always staring at that card?" he says.

I shut the binder.

"I don't know."

"I mean, aren't kids your age supposed to be looking at pictures of Britney Spears or something?"

Britney Spears is definitely okay and all but I don't

exactly see the point of a guy like me thinking about a girl like her. But I figure this is probably as good a time as any to ask Jake stuff about girls, in particular about how a person starts talking to one, like, for instance, Martha MacDowell. I want to tell him about how she smells like clean laundry and about how her hair looks like butterscotch syrup, but that sounds like I think she's a pile of clothes or a maybe a dessert.

"Hey, Jake," I say. "What does a person do if he wants another person, like maybe someone in that person's grade, to talk to him?"

Jake frowns at me. "You just talk."

I decide to get more specific. "What if the person gives you a certain look?"

He gives *me* a certain look—like I'm an idiot.

"You know, not a normal look," I say. "A look that might mean something."

"Tobe," he says. "I have no idea what you're talking about."

The next thing I know he's putting on his jean jacket. He opens his bottom dresser drawer, pulls out a small plastic bag, and kicks the drawer shut with his foot.

He's partway out the front door when I run to the top of the steps and yell out to him.

"What do you want?" he says.

I don't know what I want, but I clear my throat like I'm about to deliver the State of the Union address. Then I stand there and say exactly nothing.

Jake turns to leave.

"Where're you going?" I say.

Jake scans the street. "Out."

"On a school night?" Somehow I've turned into our mom, except not even she says anything that lame.

He opens the plastic bag, pulls out a tiny blue pill and sets it on his tongue.

"What's that?"

Jake doesn't say anything.

"What did you just take?"

He sticks out his tongue where the little blue pill is dissolving. "Acid."

Taking acid, I know from Mr. Fontaine's videos, is a lot worse than getting stoned. People on acid walk out of thirty-six-story windows or dive into pools with no water or step in front of Mack trucks. The car alarm is blaring so loud I can hardly think but I make a grab for Jake's arm, planning to put him in a headlock until he spits it out.

Except that he sidesteps me and my hand just grabs thin air. Then he's gone and I'm looking at him through the window as he steps over Tonto and crosses the parking lot.

There's nothing to do except go back upstairs and watch Eli watch TV.

It's quiet and creepy with just the two of us home. Eli turns around and looks at me. "Where is everybody?"

I shrug.

Eli wraps his blankie around his shoulders and starts to put his thumb in his mouth. He stops, though, when he realizes I'm looking at him.

I don't quite know what to do, but I know it should be some sort of big-brother-role-model-type thing. "You wanna play Nintendo?"

"You'll give me a head start?" he says. You can tell he's sort of embarrassed to have to ask on account of him liking to think he's just as good as me.

"Sure."

He puts on his cowboy hat, which he says is for good luck, hands me the controller, and we start playing. Except that I'm only playing with the half of my brain that's not wondering if Jake's okay and where our mom is and what's going on around here.

So I forget to let Eli get ahead of me and I win.

Eli gets up and switches off the game. Then he

pulls his yellow blankie over his head. Which means he's probably under there sucking his thumb. Which makes me feel like a complete jerk for making an eight-year-old so stressed out that he's back to sucking his thumb under his blankie.

"Eli," I say, addressing the yellow blankie. "I'm sorry."

The blankie doesn't respond.

"I, uh, Jeez," I say. "I forgot."

Still no answer.

I lift up a corner of the blankie and put my head underneath. The world inside is dark and warm and soft and you can see why a person would go in there if someone who promised to let him win at Nintendo just clobbered him.

"Really," I say. "I'm sorry."

He looks at me like he hopes I'm sorry but like he's not quite sure.

"I owe you a do-over," I say. "Two laps head start."

Eli perks up. "Three?"

"Okay," I say. "Three."

"One hand behind your back?"

I put my hand behind my back.

Then we both come out from under the blankie and try to act like things are normal. Except you can tell Eli doesn't really relax till he's about 185 laps ahead of me.

He pumps his skinny little arms in the air when he crosses the finish line. "Again?" he says. "Wanna do it again?"

I don't, but I do, just because he gets such a kick out of winning, even with a no-fail head start.

After about 185 more races, he puts down the controller and looks at me. "Toby," he says. "Can I ask you something?"

I use a big-brotherly-sounding voice. "Sure."

"The Easter Bunny," he says. "It's really Mom, isn't it?"

I do the only thing a person can do at a time like this: I stall. "Who told you that?"

"Jimmy Badowski."

Paul Badowski's the one who told me back in first grade; the whole family is a bunch of holiday wreckers, if you ask me.

"Well, who's he?" I say. "Encyclopedia Britannica?" Which is not only *not* the kind of thing an older big-brotherly-role-model-type person would say, it's more like the completely lame kind of thing someone Eli's age would say.

He looks sort of worried.

Which makes two of us. This being one of those once-in-a-lifetime childhood moments that can easily become one of those once-in-a-lifetime childhood traumas, I try to think of some wise, mysterious, not-technically-truthful-but-not-technically-not-truthful things people say on the Hallmark Channel.

"I believe in him," I say.

"You do?"

I nod. "Like I believe in electricity." I get up and turn the light switch off, then on.

You can tell Eli doesn't get it.

"The Easter Bunny is one of those things you can believe in even if you don't see them."

Which isn't exactly the profound, mysterious Yoda-type way Mr. D said it, but which seems to convince Eli, or which at least seems to make him feel better, since now he's looking at me like I might actually be a sort of role model big brother for once. And for once, I actually feel like I am.

I let Eli watch TV an hour past his bedtime, read him two stories, and scratch his back. After he's asleep, I go downstairs and wander around the house. I stop by the Implosion picture in the den. As usual, it's facedown so I turn it faceup. Then I go sit on the bottom step and look out the window next to the door and play a game with myself about who'll get home first.

I'll know it's my mom if a pair of headlights come straight toward the house then turn off, because that'll mean she's parking in ye olde parking space in front of our apartment. Which means I'll have to tell her that some kid in Jake's class who's sick with pneumonia and whose mother can't drive called and asked Jake to walk over the notes for the chemistry test tomorrow.

And I'll know it's Jake if the headlights beam across the front yard, then stop sideways in front of our apartment, because that'll mean someone's dropping him off by ye olde curb. Which means I'm going to tell him I'm not going to keep coming up with bogus stories about why he's throwing up or why he's not home.

Every time I see headlights I make a bet with myself. Ten points if it turns out to be Jake, negative ten if it's my mom, one point if it's nobody. By 11:32, the nobodies have 14 points. Finally, a pair of headlights beam across the yard, and a car stops at the curb and lets someone out. I run upstairs.

"I know you're not asleep," Jake says when he comes into our room.

I don't move.

"I saw you at the window, Dillweed."

I tell him to shut up or else he'll wake Eli.

"Where do you think Mom is?" It isn't what I mean to say, it's just what comes out.

He doesn't answer. It seems to take all his attention just to unbutton his shirt.

"Where's Mom?" I say.

Jake leans into my bunk. His eyes are red like the wolves' eyes on the Nature Channel. He smacks his lips and rubs his belly. It's an old joke from when I was little and I'd ask where our mom was and Jake would pretend he'd eaten her. I hated it then; I hate it worse now. I roll over to face the wall. A minute later, I roll back the other way.

"Where'd you go?" I say.

"Nowhere." He's finally gotten his shirt off and I notice that he has chest hair.

"I'm telling," I say.

"Okay," he says. "So tell."

Then he turns off the light and climbs up past me onto the top bunk. I reach up and tighten the bolt that attaches his bunk to the frame, which is something I always do before I go to sleep just to make sure his bunk doesn't fall on me and crush me in the middle of the night. A few minutes later, the front door opens and our mother comes in, humming.

The next day I get to Human Sexuality class ten minutes early so I can get a seat in the row closest to the door. This way when Nurse Wesley begins the safe sex banana demonstration and I get an emergency attack of dermatitis or whooping cough or something I can make a quick getaway. I slink down in my seat, get my baseball cap out of my backpack, pull it down over my eyes, and pray that maybe there'll be an emergency pep rally or a flood or something so we don't have to watch Nurse Wesley get romantic with a piece of fruit.

Someone taps me on the head. It's Mr. Miller, the principal, who for the first time in my life I'm actually happy to see. Since wearing a hat in school is technically a violation of the dress code, maybe he'll send me to the office or the guidance counselor. Then I won't have to come down with dermatitis or whooping cough after all.

"Malone?" he says.

I nod.

"Jake's brother?"

I nod again.

"Take that hat off," he says. He starts to walk to the front of the room, then he turns around and studies me. "You keep your nose clean," he says.

I wonder for a minute if this is a hygiene-type comment, but the way he says it, it seems more like one of those you're-skating-on-thin-ice comments that grown-ups make to kids that only make kids feel like they're in trouble without knowing exactly what they did wrong.

I agree to keep my nose clean and wait for him to send me to the office. Instead, he tells me to take a seat up front. As other people come in, he tells us the girls have gone next door to meet privately with Nurse Wesley so we can talk, "man to man."

Then he gets all groovy on us, saying it's our time to "rap." He makes flying quotation marks with his hands and pronounces the word rap like he's in a spelling bee, very *slowly* and *distinctly*.

"Not like Eminem," he says, obviously very proud of himself for knowing a pop culture person. "This kind of 'rapping,'" he says, "is something we did back in the '60s when I was your age and full of raging hormones."

I try not to get a mental picture of this.

"A 'rap' session," he says, "is where you feel free to 'let it all hang out.'" I cringe and wait for him to break out the Lava lamp and the disco music.

People squirm around in their seats. Someone in

the back of the room coughs. But no one has anything they want to "rap" with Mr. Miller about, which, to tell you the truth, makes me feel sort of bad for him since that leaves him standing in front of a bunch of kids, straightening his tie over and over again and saying embarrassing things about how sex can be beautiful in a committed relationship like the one he has with Mrs. Miller. This is an even worse mental picture than Mr. Miller and his raging hormones.

The only good thing is that he lets us go early. In the stampede out of class, Arthur grabs me by the back of my shirt.

"I thought you said Miller was gonna put a condom on a banana," he says in a not-very-quiet whisper.

A couple people turn around and look at me. I consider trying to explain to Arthur that it wasn't Mr. Miller who was going to put a condom on a banana, that it was Nurse Wesley and that it wasn't me who said so, it was Jake. Instead, I tell him to shut up and go get his stuff for tryouts.

We're late since Arthur can't find his glove, which means that we're the last ones crossing the parking lot on the way to the field, which means we're also too late to accidentally possibly see the girls' team and possibly

Martha MacDowell and her ponytail also crossing the parking lot.

What we see instead is Jake and Andy Timmons and his goatee leaning up against a car. Andy Timmons is wearing sunglasses and taking a drag on a cigarette that he's got not-so-secretly cupped inside his hand. And Jake's looking at the baseball team walking past right in front of him like it has nothing to do with him, like he didn't single-handedly clinch the division championship last year, and like he isn't the kind of player that new kid wannabes like me and Arthur and Badowski would do anything to be.

From a couple feet behind me, Coach Gillis yells out, "Malone!"

I turn around so fast I practically sprain my neck. Then, as he walks right past me like I don't exist, I realize he means Jake.

Coach Gillis shoots Andy Timmons a glance, then looks Jake up and down.

"Just what the hell do you think you're doing?"

Jake shrugs. "Nothing," he says.

"Did you forget that today's the last day of tryouts?"

"Not exactly." For about a split second Jake looks like he's nervous, like he suddenly remembered that Coach Gillis was the guy who stayed after practice a bunch of times last year to personally show him how to straighten out his swing, and who let him keep his uniform jersey to celebrate winning the division even though it was technically against the rules. Jake looks down at the ground, then over at Andy Timmons, who's grinding his cigarette out under his boot and not even pretending to be nervous. Then he looks back at Coach Gillis.

"I'm done with baseball," he says.

Coach Gillis keeps staring at Jake. He swings his whistle around till the cord is wrapped all the way up his finger, then he swings it in the other direction. When it's all the way unwrapped, he bites it between his teeth, shakes his head, and walks away.

Which means I'm standing there in the middle of the parking lot feeling weird and embarrassed and wondering what a person's supposed to do in a situation like this.

It's sort of like the time Arthur and his dad and I were leaving the movies at the mall and I spotted my dad driving the trash sweeper—this giant yellow truck with big noisy brushes that you can't help but notice. When I realized it was my dad driving, I made a big deal out of *not* noticing.

So I pull the brim of my cap so far down I practically can't see where I'm going and keep walking.

When I get to the field, I can see the kid with the pulled hamstring, who is named Sean and who I now remember was sort of annoyed last year about Jake getting MVP instead of him, already putting on the catcher's equipment in an obvious way. So I go join the other wannabes in the Outer Mongolia part of the field and wait for no one to watch us.

Except that after about twenty minutes, Coach Gillis comes over and stands at the head of our line and watches us. Which means I start sucking. Arthur throws me a soft grounder, which somehow disappears right through my glove. Then, after I run out to Outer Outer Mongolia where it rolled off to, I throw it back to him except that I practically hit Badowski in the head.

Coach Gillis comes up to me not looking exactly ecstatic. "Malone?" he says. "You gonna live up to your brother's potential?"

I've heard the legend about Coach Gillis picking some kid up by the jock strap and hanging him on a hook in the locker room, so I say yes, even though I have no idea how one person can live up to another person's potential.

"You keep your nose clean then," he says.

Behind the coach's back, Arthur's trying to make me laugh by shoving his finger up his nose. I ignore him and tell Coach Gillis I'll try, while I wonder what it is about grown-ups and kids' noses being kept clean. I also wonder what Mr. Miller and Coach Gillis know about Jake and how they know it, and if that means other people know it, too.

Arthur's mom is waiting to pick him up after practice for an orthodontist appointment, which is sort of good because it means I don't have to talk to him about Jake's showdown with Coach Gillis, but which is also sort of bad since there's no one to ride home on the late bus with. Except that when I get on, I see Martha MacDowell sitting there in her baseball cap by herself.

I decide to just sort of accidentally sit next to her like it's no big deal, like it's the kind of thing that can just happen without a person especially meaning for it to happen. Except that somehow when the moment comes to actually sit down, I end up walking right past her. The only other seat left is next to Chrissy Russo. Which is sort of a drag since I know from her being my partner last semester in Biology lab that all she likes to do is talk about Kurt Cobain, which means that as soon as the bus gets to the first stop, I decide to get off and go hang out with Mr. D instead.

He shuffles over to the counter and throws me a pack of WarHeads as soon as I walk in. "How's the Stargell?" he says.

We call the cards "the Clemente" or "the Parker," like they're things, which technically they are, but Mr. D and I also talk about them like they're people, which, if you think about it, they are. The Stargell in particular.

To tell you the truth, I *love* the Stargell, the way my dad used to love the guys at the mill and the long-lost Lucky, the wonder dog. But I'm not exactly the kind of person who says that kind of thing out loud to another person.

"It's awesome," I say, which is lame, and doesn't come anywhere close to saying how awesome it really is.

Mr. D smiles in a way that you can tell he knows exactly what I mean, then he goes back to talking online to a guy in Arkansas who has a Dino Rostelli rookie card for sale.

I wander over and stand behind him to see what the guy from Arkansas is asking for the Rostelli. I clear my throat.

"Why are grown-ups always telling kids to keep their noses clean?"

I figure Mr. D, who practically wrote the playbook on mysterious cornball sayings, will know what I'm talking about.

And unlike typical grown-ups who say they're busy or don't even hear you when you ask them something personal, Mr. D stops what he's doing and turns around and looks at me.

"When someone says to keep your nose clean, they're telling you to stay out of trouble," he says, which is a surprisingly normal, non-Yodalike answer for him.

"Mr. D?" I don't exactly know what I'm going to say, but Mr. D looks at me like he thinks it might be something important. "What do you do if you're worried about someone doing something they shouldn't be doing?"

He doesn't answer right away.

"Something that if they get caught might make other people upset," I say.

He cocks his head to the side. "You're worried about this person?"

"I guess."

"Do you think that'll help?"

I don't understand.

"Worrying," he says. "Does it help?"

I think the answer is yes, but I can tell from the way he's asking it, the answer's supposed to be no. I shrug.

"Toby," he says, "worrying is a waste of time and energy. It doesn't rob tomorrow of its sting. It only robs today of its strength."

This is probably his Zen-Yoda way of telling me to chill, but, even though he doesn't mean to, it makes me feel sort of like an idiot. Which I am a lot of times, but not usually when I'm with Mr. D. Which makes me feel like an even bigger idiot.

I also think, maybe for the first time in my life, that Mr. D might possibly be wrong. You're *supposed* to worry about someone who's doing something they're not supposed to do. You've got to, otherwise something will happen and things won't ever be the same. I don't tell Mr. D this, though. I don't say anything on account of feeling partly idiotic and partly bummed out about Mr. D not understanding about why a person needs to worry.

At which point he tosses me another pack of WarHeads. Which is at least something.

At dinner that night, while our mom is in the kitchen getting out the food—Food King crab cakes and fries—I kick Jake under the table.

"Thanks a lot," I say.

He just looks at me.

"You told me Nurse Wesley was gonna put a condom on a banana," I say.

"So?"

"So, she didn't."

"So?"

"So I told Arthur that she was, and he told other people and then when we had a 'rap' session with Mr. Miller instead, I looked like a complete moron."

He laughs. "You believed that?"

I did. I believed him. "Not really," I say.

"What's a condom?" says Eli.

We ignore him.

"Did Miller tell you about the '60s and him being full of raging hormones?" Jake says.

"Yeah."

"Did he tell you about sex being a beautiful thing?"

"Sex!" Eli says. "You said sex!"

I smile. I can't help it. Just like the other day—I mean to be mad at Jake but somehow I'm not. "Yeah," I say, "when it's in a relationship like the one he has with Mrs. Miller."

We're both laughing now. Jake's slapping his hand on his thigh like he did when the Pissing-Off-the-

World kid was covered with red dots. Eli keeps asking what's so funny, and our mom comes in with the food, not looking like she has a terminal headache, smiling that cornball smile moms smile when their kids are getting along and not throwing sofa pillows at each other.

And it's sort of like the old days, which makes me wonder if Mr. D might possibly be right about not worrying so much.

About halfway through dinner, my mom, as usual, asks how school was. And, as usual, I answer with some little factoid, on account of her bursting into tears one night right after our dad left, when she asked how school was and nobody said anything. So I tell her about the math teacher having a new baby, which happened a while ago but which I was saving for when I needed it. Eli tells her that his class is having a Save the Pandas bake sale. Jake doesn't say anything.

"How's baseball going?" She addresses this question to me and Jake but Jake's not looking at her.

"Coach Gillis is trying me out for backup catcher." I sound sort of loud, even to myself.

Jake looks up. And all of a sudden I feel sort of embarrassed. Embarrassed about how totally psyched I am about something he's obviously now too cool for. And also sort of embarrassed for him, for not already knowing about me possibly being backup catcher, and finding out at dinner in front of our mom and Eli instead of on the field like he normally would have.

"How about you, Jake?" she says. "Are you playing shortstop or whatever it was you were last year?"

Jake sort of grunts, then he grabs a bunch of fries.

"You're awfully hungry," she says.

He shovels the fries in his mouth.

"Coach Gillis must be working you pretty hard."

Jake sort of half nods. Our mom scrunches her eyebrows together.

So I jump in. "Badowski caught an amazing pop fly today," I announce. "Off Arthur's last at-bat."

She just looks at me.

"And the coach taught us some new signals today. This—" I tap out a bunch of bogus signs Jake and I made up back in our Little League days. "This means bunt, and this"—I pull on my ear and tug on an imaginary hat—"means sacrifice."

You can tell she doesn't know quite how to deal with suddenly having Bob Costas at the dinner table. "That's nice," she says finally. She sounds small, the way she does whenever we talk about sports, and I feel sort of bad.

When she gets up to get dessert, Jake looks over my

way and winks. I'm pretty sure it's his way of saying thanks for not busting him on not going out for baseball. Which means I'm finally doing something he considers cool, which normally would've made me feel good, but actually makes me feel surprisingly rotten.

So I get up, give Eli my dessert, and go upstairs and stare at the Stargell for a while.

After dinner, when I come downstairs to ask my mom about getting new cleats, I see her sitting at the kitchen table, counting the money from her tip jar. Little towers of quarters and dimes and nickels are stacked up in front of a bunch of wrinkled bills and she's counting the money over and over, like if she counts it one more time, it'll add up to more. She gets up and feels around in her bathrobe pocket for her new herbal stop-smoking gum, and I slink back up the steps.

Later, after everyone else is in bed, I can't sleep so I go downstairs to get a bowl of Lucky Charms. I pick up the mail and sift through it for any personal stuff, like a letter or a postcard from California. But there's nothing but bills and junk mail. I set aside two envelopes, though: an American Express bill marked "Second Notice" and an envelope stamped with the words "You may have already won!" I slip the bill in my back pocket, pour out the Lucky Charms, and sit down and rip open the you-may-have-already-won envelope.

With the purchase of just three magazine subscriptions, the people from the you-may-have-already-won contest say we'll be entered in a drawing, where the grand prize is one million dollars. There's no obligation; the subscriptions can be canceled at any time.

So I order a subscription to *Cooking Lite* for my mom, *Sports Illustrated* for me and Jake, and *National Geographic Kids* for Eli. Then I check off the "Bill Me Later" box, sign my name right above where it says "Open to contestants over age 21," and make a note to myself to cancel the magazines if we don't win.

The next afternoon, as soon as the last bell rings, Arthur and I meet up to walk down to the locker room to see if by some miracle our names are on the list of people who made it for the team. We walk slow at first, then faster, then slow again, speeding up and slowing down depending on how hopeful or hopeless we are as we try to figure out our chances.

When we get there, I'm too nervous to look. Which is okay because Arthur, who never gets nervous about anything, says he'll look for both of us.

A bunch of guys are crowded around the locker-room door. Arthur pushes his way to the front, then starts jumping up and down so he can see the list, his flaming red hair appearing and disappearing in between all the shoulders of the guys who are older and taller. Then I hear him whoop. Then he hollers. Then he bursts out of the crowd and does a backflip, which he knows how to do from fourth grade when his mom made him take gymnastics. Which, of course, is highly embarrassing, but which means we made it.

But which I won't actually believe until I see the list, too.

I inch my way through the crowd, which is now actually two crowds: the guys who are thumping each other on the head because they made it, and the guys who are watching guys thump each other on the head because they didn't make it. They step aside so I can see the list.

And my name is right on it. Which makes it official that I'm on the team.

And which also makes it official that Jake's not.

"We made it!" Arthur says. His face is almost as red as his hair. "We made it."

"Yeah," I say. I mean to sound happy, which I am, but I end up sounding bummed out, which I also am. "Yeah," I say again.

At which point, a bunch of girls go by, including Martha MacDowell.

"We made the team," Arthur yells out. "Me and Toby."

The girls look at Arthur the way girls usually look at Arthur—like he's entertaining as long as he's at a safe distance.

Then Martha MacDowell looks at me and smiles. It's an actual, no-doubt-about-it smile that isn't pitying or kindhearted or anything except normal.

"Congratulations," she says. "What position do you play?"

I don't say anything. Sometimes around girls I act like I have the IQ of a paramecium. This is one of those times.

Arthur elbows me in the rib. "Catcher," he says. "He plays catcher."

"Me too," she says.

I nod. Then I swallow. Then I clear my throat, like I have something to say. Which I don't.

Then Martha MacDowell does give me a pitying look, the kind you give someone who's suddenly been hit with an acute case of mental retardation.

Badowski comes over and thumps me on the head—so hard that if I didn't have an acute case of mental retardation before, I definitely do now.

Then Martha MacDowell and the other girls are walking away, and Arthur and Badowski are talking about what a great team it's gonna be. Meanwhile, I'm trying to decide what's the matter with a person who can get a Stargell rookie card, make the baseball team, and have a good-smelling girl smile at him, and still not feel like thumping people on the head or getting thumped on the head.

I'm a couple blocks away from school when a white car drives past, slams on the brakes, and backs up till it's right next to me. Andy Timmons and his goatee are in the driver's seat and the rest of the car is full of kids I sort of recognize from school, including the Pissing-Off-the-World kid, and a girl with spiky black hair, who's in one of my study halls but who always sleeps through it.

Andy Timmons sticks his head out the window and asks if I want a ride.

"No, thanks." I sound like Miss Manners.

"Hey, Toby!" I hear Jake's voice from somewhere in the backseat. Then he leans across the seat in front of a blond-haired girl and sticks his head out the window. "C'mon. Get in."

"That's okay."

The door opens and a couple of empty beer cans fall out.

"Get in," says Andy Timmons.

The whole thing feels like one of Mr. Fontaine's peer pressure videos, where the low self-esteem kid goes along with the cool kids and ruins his life because he can't say no. So I shake my head. Then the blond-haired girl, who I recognize from the lunchroom from wearing really short skirts and having teeth like a movie star and who I secretly think looks like Britney Spears, maybe even prettier, leans out the back window.

"Is that your little brother?" she says to Jake. "He's so *cute*." She makes it sound like I'm a pet gerbil or something. "What grade are you in?" she says to me.

I have another attack of sudden retardation.

When I don't say anything, she turns to Jake. "What grade is he in?"

"Freshman," Jake says. "He's only thirteen, though. He's a brainiac. He skipped a grade when he was little."

Andy Timmons guns the motor. "Get in, brainiac."

Then the blond-haired girl pats the spot on the seat next to her, and the next thing I know I'm sitting in the back of Andy Timmons's car, practically touching her.

I try to think of something to say, but the only thing that comes to mind is how the chicken à la king school lunch that day looked exactly like Mr. Furry's Fancy Feast Chicken Dinner. But even in my suddenly retarded condition, I know that's not exactly a suave and sophisticated conversation starter. The only other thing that occurs to me is to tell her that she's got the best teeth of anyone I've ever had the privilege of sitting near in my entire life. Instead, I say absolutely nothing and sit there like a box of frozen Food King appetizers.

I can see, even from the backseat, that Andy Timmons is driving fifty-seven miles an hour, which is twenty-two miles an hour faster than the speed limit, but I don't say anything. I don't even say anything when he drives right past the turnoff for the highway, or when he turns onto Creekside Road, this windy road in the complete opposite direction of our house.

I'm just sitting like a frozen mini-quiche when Andy Timmons starts jerking the steering wheel from side to side. The car swerves into the other lane, then swerves back into the lane we were supposed to be in. One minute I'm practically sitting on the blond girl's lap, the next minute I'm being bashed into the door. I jam the lock down with my elbow and pray for him to stop. Or at least for everyone else in the car to stop laughing.

The blond girl smiles a future-movie-star smile at me. "Don't worry, Jake's little brother," she says. "We do this all the time."

I nod like I do this kind of thing all the time, too. Then I yell "Look out!" right in Andy Timmons's ear. Since he's busy flipping through his CD case, he doesn't see the Wonder Bread truck coming straight at us. He yanks the wheel to the right. Which means we don't die in a tragic head-on collision with a bread truck, but which means we end up on the side of the road in the grass.

Which is when everybody stops laughing.

"Nice going, brainiac." This comes from Vince, the Pissing-Off-the-World kid, who isn't exactly a member of the National Honor Society, if you know what I mean.

Jake grabs the brim of my baseball cap and jams it down over my eyes. I can feel the blond girl shift around in her seat so she isn't touching me anymore.

I yank my hat off and see that Andy Timmons is pulling something out of his jacket pocket.

I've never seen a joint in real life before, only laminated pictures like the ones Mr. Fontaine passed around during Freedom From Chemical Dependency Week. It's surprisingly small.

Jake's friends each take turns smoking it and passing it around, including the blond girl, who inhales like she's kissing. Then she holds the joint out in my direction, her mouth still all kissy holding in the smoke.

"That's okay," I say, waving my hands through the air in front of me.

She keeps holding it out toward me. Vince and the spiky-haired girl are looking at me.

I morph into Miss Manners again. "No, thank you," I say.

Finally, she exhales. "Pass it, will you?"

I realize they're all waiting for me—not to succumb to peer pressure and ruin my entire life—just to pass it along so they can keep smoking. So even though I keep expecting a helicopter full of FBI agents in navy blue windbreakers to parachute onto the hood, point their semiautomatic machine guns at me, and haul me off to prison, I take the thing from her.

I plan to hold it the way Jake did, pinching it between his thumb and index finger, but somehow I end up holding it between my first two fingers, the way little kids do when they fake-smoke with pretzels. It weighs practically nothing. Still, I keep picturing myself accidentally dropping it and setting the car on fire and killing everyone, which would be just the kind of tragic surprise ending that always happens in Mr. Fontaine's videos.

But nothing happens. They smoke the joint down to nothing. Then Andy Timmons pulls back onto the road, driving a little fast but mainly normally, and not showing any signs of impaired reflexes or hand-eye coordination. Vince puts in a new CD, which the girl with the movie-star teeth and the spiky-haired girl sing along to. And Jake doesn't look any different than he does when we watch TV alone together after school.

All of this strikes me as sort of weird but I still don't relax. Not until we get home and I can see that my mom's car isn't in the lot.

I jump out of the car, thank Andy Timmons for the ride—even if he did just about get me killed by a bread truck—and run inside and grab the Citrus Magic and spray it all over myself.

After I'm done, I bring the Citrus Magic into the den for Jake, who's sitting on the floor playing with Mr. Furry. Some hip-hop song is on MTV, and Jake has Mr. Furry standing up on her hind legs, holding on to her front paws, making her dance in time with the music.

"Mr. Furry," he says. "The J.Lo of cats."

He pulls her paws back and forth and makes her hips swivel, which I have to admit actually makes her look like a short, hairy Jennifer Lopez with a tail.

When he sees me watching, he makes Mr. Furry take a bow.

I smile, sort of, even though I don't want him to think I've forgotten about him and his friends practically getting me imprisoned for life. But it also cracks me up seeing Mr. Furry, who's so stuck-up, looking so miserable.

Then the front door opens and our mom and Eli walk in carrying bags of groceries. I jump up, shove the Citrus Magic under the couch, and go to help my mom put the food away.

I'm stacking up the cans of tuna next to the boxes of Tuna Helper, when my mom wrinkles her nose. "It smells in here," she says.

I don't move.

She sniffs. She looks around the kitchen, her eyebrows all scrunched up.

"It smells like oranges," she says, looking at me. "Toby, were you two drinking Sunkist before dinner?"

I pretend I don't hear her.

"Toby?" she says.

I swallow.

Then Jake calls out to her from the den. "Hey, Ma!" he says. "C'mere. Watch this."

"Mommy," yells Eli. "Come look."

She gives up on being Sherlock Holmes and goes into the den. I follow her. Jake's on the floor making Mr. Furry do a ghetto move where you wag your fingers in time with music and Eli's trying to make rap sounds but is mainly just spitting.

I look over at my mom, who isn't a big rap fan, but she's smiling.

I edge up next to her. "Mr. Furry," I say. "The J.Lo of cats." She rolls her eyes, but you can tell it cracks her up. She shakes her head and goes back into the kitchen.

When she's gone, I walk across the room and turn the Implosion picture faceup. Then I flop down onto the couch, even though what I really want to do is lie down in my bunk and curl up into a fetal position and go to sleep for the rest of my life.

That night, I figure, is as good a time as any. Eli's asleep, and Jake and I are lying in the dark after our mom came in and made us turn off the light.

"Can I ask you something, Jake?"

He doesn't say no. So I ask.

"What's it like?"

"What's what like?"

"You know." I exhale. "Pot."

He doesn't say anything right away.

"It's amazing." He sounds like he used to when he talked about people like Mark McGwire or Cal Ripken or Derek Jeter. "Totally amazing."

That's not what Mr. Fontaine's videos say. "Really?" I try hard to sound casual.

"Really," Jake says. "I mean, everything's different. Everything's okay when you're stoned. Things that aren't funny are funny. Things that suck don't suck. Everything's better. Everything."

Up till now it hadn't occurred to me that anything sucked for Jake.

"But it's nothing compared to acid," he says. "You can see things, really see things, on acid."

I wonder why people on acid can't see Mack trucks coming at them or see that they're stepping out of thirty-six-story windows. "But it's really bad for you, isn't it?"

Jake snorts. "Big Macs are bad for you. Listening to the headphones with the volume all the way is up is bad for you. According to Mom, everything's bad for you."

I kick the covers off and flip my pillow over to the other side where it's still cool. "But what if you get caught?" I say. "Mom'll lose it."

"I'm not gonna get caught. I never get caught."

"But it's against the law." All of a sudden I'm Judge Judy.

"Jeez, Toby, don't be such a narc."

I reach up and tighten the bolt on the board under Jake's mattress.

"It's just, you know . . ." I don't know how to finish. "I just don't want anything bad to happen to you."

"Toby." He sighs. "You're such a dillweed." He says dillweed the old way, not the way he said it in front of Andy Timmons the other day. "Nothing's gonna happen."

In PE the next day, Nurse Wesley, who's somehow subbing for Coach Gillis, announces that we're going to play this Colonial America game where the girls have to take off one of their shoes and put it in a pile in the middle of the gym floor, and the boys have to pick a shoe out of the pile and go around and match it up with the right girl, then hold her hand while we do a Colonial American–type square dance.

I decide then that I will definitely not live till the end of PE, let alone live long enough to go through puberty.

So while Nurse Wesley's spelling out the rules of

the game, I memorize what kind of shoes Chrissy Russo's wearing. Not because I want to have physical contact with Chrissy Russo or anything, but because if I'm going to have to have physical contact with a girl, I want it to be a girl who at least likes people who are alive.

So as soon as Nurse Wesley blows the whistle for us to run to the shoe pile, I elbow the people next to me out of the way, which isn't too hard since none of the boys are too hot to play, and make a grab for the first shoe that isn't Chrissy's.

Which turns out to be Martha MacDowell's.

Who walks up to me, smiles, takes her shoe, and puts it on. Then, she actually, physically holds my hand. After which I wait to die.

"So," she says all casual, like having actual physical contact is completely normal, and not something that only happens to the people in our Human Sexuality videos, "you play catcher, right?"

I nod and mentally congratulate myself for at least being able to work my head even if the rest of my body has already gone into rigor mortis.

"So who do you think's better? Jason Kendall or Josh Fogg?"

"Definitely Jason Kendall," I say.

The answer just comes out, since everyone knows Jason Kendall is better than Josh Fogg. And I wonder if this is what people are talking about when they say they're having an out-of-body experience right before they die. Because even though my body is there in the gym listening to Nurse Wesley yelling out Colonial American dance commands, my mind is somewhere in the top row of the bleachers, watching the person who's me down on the gym floor talking to Martha MacDowell, and actually having physical contact with her and not dying.

At which point I realize that I'm not only not dying, I'm actually sort of liking it. Because Martha MacDowell turns out to be a girl who actually wants to talk baseball, and whose hand is smaller than mine and sort of soft and not sweaty at all.

And I'm not sure, but I think it's possible that she doesn't mind holding hands with me either since she doesn't try to run away the minute Nurse Wesley says we have to change partners.

The next night, to celebrate making the team, Arthur invites me over for dinner. Which is cool because his mom makes really good things like meat loaf and meatballs and other real-mom foods, but which is not something I do very often since his whole family is really out there with their feelings, which is fun but which tires me out by the time we get to dessert.

Mrs. Lucarelli kisses me hello. She always does this even though she always says she knows she's not supposed to, but which she says can't help.

"I don't mind," I say, which is true. I don't. I like how she smells like a real kitchen and how she laughs at stuff that isn't even funny.

Then Mr. Lucarelli, who talks to me like I'm a real person and not some dweeb friend of his son, says Arthur told him about me getting the Stargell.

And instead of getting an attack of mental retardation like I normally do, I get brainiac's disease. I tell him all about the '79 World Series clutch homer and about Stargell still holding the team record for home runs (475) and grand slams (11) and about Mr. D being sort of like Yoda in a Mister Rogers sweater. Until I finally realize that I've been talking for about 185 hours.

Mr. Lucarelli just smiles. "You . . ." he says, pausing for dramatic effect, "are one lucky son of a gun."

He puts his hand out for me to shake.

It's not the manly man's no-shake handshake; it's more like a business handshake. It's probably the handshake he uses at his office job all the time but not something he generally uses with kids, except maybe when they have a once-in-a-lifetime thing happen to them. Which makes me feel kind of embarrassed but also definitely kind of proud.

Mrs. Lucarelli comes out of the kitchen with the lasagna.

"I know it's your favorite," she says.

I wonder how she knows it's my favorite without *me* even knowing it's my favorite. She probably just figured it out from all the times I've eaten there. And come to think of it, it probably *is* my favorite.

So I say thanks. Then we all sit down and I make a big deal out of liking her lasagna.

Mr. and Mrs. Lucarelli ask typical parental questions like which kid in our class do we think could end up being president some day, and which teachers do we like best. Arthur and I do our best to dodge their questions without actually looking like we're dodging them.

"So . . ." Mr. Lucarelli says when we're done. "How about a little karaoke?"

For a half second I think this is some kind of foreign food that Mrs. Lucarelli made for dessert. Then I realize that he's talking about this highly embarrassing thing where people pretend to be rock stars by singing into a microphone while a machine plays backup music.

Mrs. Lucarelli claps her hands like a little kid. Mr. Lucarelli gets out of his chair and does a not-too-bad-for-someone's-dad moon walk. And Arthur looks at me the way Harriet the Horrible used to look at me when she wanted to play ball.

And I just sit there and wonder what you can possibly say to people who make your favorite dinner and give you a once-in-a-lifetime handshake and share their Little Debbies with you, when the last thing in the world you want to do is sing karaoke.

I hate karaoke. Not only is it way too out-there emotionally for someone like me, it's sort of cheesy, especially if you do it in your basement after dinner and not on a reality TV show or something.

I swallow. "I can't," I say, which is true since I'd probably hyperventilate to death if I did by some miracle even try it. "We have a math test tomorrow."

Mrs. Lucarelli says she understands, and Mr. Lucarelli says it's okay, that I need to put my schoolwork first, and Arthur rolls his eyes. You can tell they're disappointed but are trying not to make me feel bad about them being disappointed.

I leave feeling pretty rotten. But not as rotten as I do when I get on my skateboard and hear them singing "Disco Inferno" from partway down the block. It makes me wish that, even though we live in a condo, that we did some kind of normal family-type thing, even if it was karaoke.

By the time I get home it's dark, and my mom's waiting at the front door, wearing her *Law & Order* dress. I call it that because she bought it to wear to court to ask the judge to make my dad send us money, which he never does. Every time she wears it I get this sort-of-nervous, sort-of-excited feeling, because I think it means my dad might show up.

"How come you're wearing that?" I say.

"Why? What's wrong with it?" She looks down at her front, like maybe she spilled something on herself and doesn't know it.

"Nothing," I say. "It's fine."

"Really?"

"Really."

She walks over to the steps, yells up to Jake and Eli to turn the TV down. Then she smoothes the dress over her stomach, puts on more lipstick, and goes back to staring out the window. "Oh no," she says. "He's here."

"He's here?" I practically knock her unconscious trying to open the door. But the man coming up the walkway isn't my dad. He's shorter than my dad, shorter and pudgy, and he's holding out a bouquet of flowers and looking like he thinks maybe he's at the wrong house.

"Well," my mom says, peeking out from behind me. "Right on time."

"Right on time," the man says. He holds the flowers out in my direction, until my mom not-so-gently pushes me out of the way.

"Oh, how sweet," she says, taking the bouquet.

"This must be your son," the man says, looking at me.

"Roses," she says, her nose stuck in the bouquet. "My favorite."

"Jake?" the man says, extending his hand.

I shake my head.

My mom elbows me in the ribs. "This is Toby," she says. "Toby, say hello to Stanley."

I take my hand out of my pocket, wave hello, then fold my arms across my chest. Stanley takes his handshake hand and runs it through his hair, his face sort of stalled in mid-smile. "Nice to meet you," he says.

"Here," she says, shoving the roses at me. "Find something to put these in, will you? We won't be late."

She turns to leave, then calls back over her shoulder and yells upstairs, "Bye, Jake. Bye, Eli." I let her kiss me, but I don't wait till she's gone to wipe off the lipstick like I usually do.

And then they're gone, and I'm standing at the front door holding Stanley's bouquet. I walk into the kitchen, stick the flowers in an old Pirates mug, and go upstairs to find out what's going on.

Jake and Eli are playing Nintendo as usual.

"Who was that?" I say.

Jake wraps Eli's blankie around his shoulders and waves it like a cape.

"His Heinie!" Eli shrieks. "Mom went on a date with His Heinie."

"That guy?" I say. "That guy's the Food King?"

Jake grins. "Yup. Master of the Mini Quiche. King of Crab Cakes."

"Mom went on an actual date?" I sit down at the desk.

They don't answer.

"Mom says he might take us to a Pirates game sometime," Eli says.

"She said he has season tickets," Jake says.

"So?" I say.

"So, I thought you liked the Pirates," Eli says.

I shrug.

I get up, then sit down again and open my card collection and stare at the Stargell. Which is the only thing a person can do at a time like this.

A couple minutes later, Jake punches Eli in the shoulder and gets up. "Ya got me again, Killer."

Eli gloats, and I wonder if he really thinks he beat Jake. He begs for another match.

But Jake goes straight for his bottom drawer and pulls out a little plastic bag. He stuffs it in his pocket and walks out. I sit there for a minute, not knowing what to do, then I hop up like a human jack-in-the-box and follow him.

When I get downstairs to the kitchen, Jake's screwing the lid back on our mom's tip jar. I feel embarrassed for him, the way you feel when you accidentally walk in on someone in the bathroom, but also mad at him for taking her tip money.

Jake turns around.

"What do you want?" he says.

"Nothing."

Jake starts to go past me.

"Where're you going?" I say.

"Nowhere," he says. "Wanna come?"

It's another old joke that isn't funny anymore.

"Seriously," he says. "You wanna come?"

"What do you mean?"

"I'm just going for a walk around the block." He pinches his fingers together and I get it; he's doing an imitation of smoking a joint.

"Nah." I back up a step. "That's okay."

"Whatever," Jake says, brushing past me, and opens the front door.

We both see that it's started raining. Jake looks annoyed, then he shuts the door, shrugs his jean jacket off onto the floor, and heads back toward the kitchen. I trot along behind him, feeling like Harriet the Horrible, not knowing exactly what else to do. He goes into the downstairs bathroom, the one my mom calls the powder room, and opens the window. He takes out a little blue pipe, which he fills with pot, and lights it. He pulls the smoke into his lungs, holds it, then sticks his head out the window and blows it out into the rain.

I reach up and turn on the fan. Then I go get the Citrus Magic.

I'm upstairs lying in my bunk, looking at the Stargell, when Eli comes and taps me on the shoulder. "Can I ask you something?" he says.

Whatever it is, I hope it's not about the Easter Bunny.

He looks worried. "It's about Mr. Furry," he says.

He waits for me to say something like I usually do about Mr. Furry being lame and stuck-up compared to Harriet the Horrible. Under the circumstances, I decide not to.

"Have you seen her lately?"

I shake my head.

"She's missing."

"So?"

"So." He pulls his blankie up around his neck. "So I'm scared."

"Don't worry," I say. "She has to be around here somewhere."

Eli shakes his head. "I think she got out. The window to the downstairs bathroom was open."

"Jake!" I yell. "Mr. Furry got out."

Now Eli looks really worried. "Jake went out," he whispers.

I slam my binder shut.

Eli jumps. Then he pulls his blankie over his head. Little sniffling sounds come from under the blankie.

I get up, squeeze the spot on the blankie that I think is his shoulder, and tell him I'll go look for Mr. Furry.

"Just so you know," I say, "I'm not doing this for Mr. Furry. I'm doing it for you."

A tiny "thanks" comes from under the blankie.

I walk up and down ye olde streets of Colonial Mews shaking a can of Liver Lovin' cat treats and calling out to Mr. Furry like she's my long-lost best friend.

"Mr. Fur-ree? Oh, Mr. Fur-ree," I sing out, feeling like a complete idiot, not to mention a complete fake.

It starts to rain again right about the time I've made my second lap around the neighborhood, but I keep going, shaking the liver treats and serenading a cat I don't even like. I pull my jacket over my head and decide to make another sweep of the parking lot, when I finally spot her under a car in the last row. I creep over to the car, shake the can of Liver Lovin' treats like bait, then charge for her and grab her by the tail. She whips around and bites me, then darts across the grass and around the corner of a row of condos.

I trot along after her, even though I'm pretty sure that chasing a stuck-up cat around in the rain is a good way of getting pneumonia. I find her a couple minutes later, hiding in a little kid's plastic playhouse in somebody's AstroTurf yard. Even though there are probably laws against trespassing in kids' playhouses, I tiptoe up to the playhouse, bend over, and sneak in. This time I don't even try to use the liver treats; I make a lunge for her. She darts out the door between my legs; I give up and start walking home.

Just as I reach for the doorknob, Mr. Furry shoots out from under the Dumpster, runs across the yard, and slips inside the door. She doesn't even look wet, she just looks annoyed, like I'd been keeping her waiting.

The next day at the end of school, I take the scenic route around the upstairs hall on the way to my locker, thinking that maybe I'll see Martha MacDowell at her locker. But by the time I get there, she's gone, which is probably good since I had no idea what I was going to do if she was there.

After that, I skateboard over to Mr. D's because I just feel like doing stuff for him, not for money even, just to hang around with somebody who's the same every time you see them and not suddenly hanging out with people who smoke pot or suddenly start dating people who star in TV commercials dressed like a member of the Royal Family.

"Toby," he says as soon as I walk in. "How ya doin'?"

Usually, when people ask you how you're doing, they don't really want to know actual details, like how you're afraid to ask your mom for new cleats. But when Mr. D asks, you know he actually wants to know.

"Okay, I guess."

Mr. D tosses me a pack of WarHeads. "You don't sound so sure."

The WarHeads are the extra-hot kind that explode on the roof of your mouth, the kind that can make your eyes get watery if you're not careful.

"I miss my dog," I tell him. "Harriet. Harriet the Horrible." This isn't what I meant to say, but it's true. "I know it sounds dumb," I said, "but I do."

Nobody else thought Harriet was so great, partly because she had really short legs and a pointy head that made her look sort of like a hyena, but mainly no one was too crazy about Harriet on account of her bad breath. But at least she was always the same. She was always glad to see you when you came home, and you could count on her to get up on the couch next to you and thump her stubby tail against your leg and smile her hyena-dog smile at you and breathe her bad breath on you no matter what.

I tell all this to Mr. D, who just stands there nodding like what I'm saying makes perfect sense.

"Son," he says after I finally shut up about how great Harriet was. "Living is all about letting go."

I don't know what he means, and to tell you the truth I'm not sure I agree, since we're both card collectors, which, if you think about it, isn't about letting go, it's about getting and keeping stuff. But I say I do, making a mental note to tuck this little bit of Yoda-type philosophy away for future use, since Mr. D seems to be so serious about it, calling me son and all.

"I know how you feel, though," he says. "Most of the time, I can let go, but some days . . ." He sighs. ". . . Some days I really miss my wife." He starts patting his back pants pocket for the old plaid handkerchief, and I realize that if I don't do something quick, things could get emotional.

"Yeah," I say. "But I bet she didn't have bad breath like Harriet."

I know, right as I'm saying it, that it's kind of politically incorrect to compare a beloved dead wife to a dog with hyena breath, but it cracks Mr. D up. He claps me on the back, gives me another pack of WarHeads, and stuffs his handkerchief back in his pocket. And I stay there till closing time, tying up the recycling, reaching up to get stuff on the top shelves where Mr. D can't reach, and feeling almost like I used to feel watching TV in the afternoons with old Harriet.

That night after hanging up the phone, my mom announces that the Food King is taking us to a Pirates game tomorrow.

I know without even checking the paper that Kip Wells is pitching, probably with Mike Williams as closer, and Pokey Reese is back in action at second base after a pulled groin—a game any kid in his right mind would want to see.

"I have to work for Mr. D that day," I say.

She gives me the maternal eyebrow scrunch, which makes me wonder if *I'm* in my right mind.

"Really," I say.

I think maybe she's about to say something, but then she unscrunches her eyebrows. "Oh, well," she says. "Okay."

Which, to tell you the truth, makes me feel worse than if she'd said "What do you mean you're not going?" which I was expecting, maybe even hoping for. Because even though I'm not sure I want to go see the Pirates with someone who's not my dad, I at least want her to ask me about not going, or maybe even try to talk me out of it and not just say okay.

The next morning, Jake keeps humming the National Anthem and saying "Play ball," the way our dad used to do; Eli keeps asking our mom if she thinks Stanley will buy him a Pirates jersey, and our mom keeps trying on different outfits, until the Food King finally pulls up in big black SUV and they all leave.

The house is instantly empty and way too quiet. I open the fridge and poke around for something to eat. I grab a piece of my mom's Weight Watchers cake, eat some of the frosting off the top, then shove it back in the fridge. I make a point of slamming the door, which feels lame and stupid and not at all impressive since there's no one around to hear it except me.

After a while, I wander into the den, turn the Implosion photo faceup, and nudge Mr. Furry out of my seat. She gives me a how-dare-you look, then saunters out of the room in her stuck-up cat way, while I turn on the TV. Which, since it's pretty much always on ESPN, means I'm sitting there watching a pregame interview with Pokey Reese, who's in the middle of saying how today's game is going to be the turning point of the season, when I snap off the TV, leaving his voice hanging in mid-word, and wonder what I'm gonna do for the rest of the day.

A couple of nights later, our mom comes home from work extra late and extra tired from having to do highlights on one of her regulars who showed up for her appointment late, and then only gave her a five-dollar tip. Jake's not home yet, which she doesn't seem to notice, the way she also doesn't notice how he comes home later than me a lot of days—even though we're both supposedly at baseball—and how there's only one uniform in the laundry every week.

"Did anyone call?" she says, meaning His Heinie.

I shake my head.

She frowns.

"Are you sure?"

"I'm sure," I say.

She nods, straightens her back a little, then puts on a smile.

"I have an idea," she says after checking in the refrigerator. "Let's order pizza."

I'd been thinking of maybe asking her to make the orange meal, which is sort of like our family's karaoke. It's a meal Jake and I invented of all orange foods—macaroni and cheese, Cheetos, mandarin oranges, and Sunkist sodas—which we used to have on special occasions, like when one of us lost a tooth or learned how to ride a two-wheeler. It wasn't a special occasion or anything. I just wanted to have something like we used to have, so maybe things would feel like they used to feel.

But when I start to ask, I can see the terminal headache look on her face.

"Pizza sounds good," I say.

She calls in the order then goes upstairs to take a shower. The Domino's delivery guy rings the doorbell while she's drying her hair.

"Toby?" she calls out from upstairs. "Reach inside my tip jar and grab some money, will you?"

I take the jar down off the top of the refrigerator and count out $7.12.

"Ma," I call up to her. "There's not enough."

The Domino's guy gives me a suspicious look and clutches his insulated red delivery pouch to his side. I'm standing there feeling like a criminal when I remember that there's only $7.12 in the jar because Jake took the rest.

"Count it again," my mom calls out. "I know I put a twenty in there."

I give the Domino's guy a just-a-minute look, then I dig around in my pocket for the money I earned at Mr. D's other day. I give him enough for the pizza plus a tip in mostly nickels, which you can tell he doesn't especially appreciate.

My mom comes downstairs and we sit down to eat, finally, and the phone rings. She grabs the receiver, then stands there letting it ring one more time before she picks it up. "I don't want to look like I was waiting for him," she says.

"No," she says into the receiver. "You're not interrupting." Then she tucks the phone under her chin, goes up to her room, and closes the door.

"Must be His Heinie," says Eli, who's wearing the Pokey Reese T-shirt "Stanley" bought him.

"It was funny the first thousand times, Eli," I say.

Eli looks at me, then opens his mouth as wide as he can so I can see his predigested pizza.

We sit there chewing, not saying anything for a couple of minutes. "Where's Jake?" Eli says after a while.

I smack my lips and rub my stomach, like I've just eaten him.

Eli rolls his eyes. "It's only funny when Jake does it," he says.

Our mom comes down wearing a dress and perfume.

"Where's Jake?" she says.

I shrug.

"Okay, Toby, you're in charge till he gets home," she says. "Make sure Eli does his homework."

Then she's gone, and Eli goes up to do his homework. Which is sort of good, because I don't have to bug him about it, but which is also sort of bad since, to tell you the truth, I could've gone for a game of Nintendo right about then.

After Eli falls asleep, I sit at the front door playing the headlight game. The nobodies have twelve points when a car pulls up and drops Jake off. He weaves up the path then stops like he's forgotten where he was going. I open the door, and he takes a step toward me, then trips, grabbing the air for something to hold on to.

I reach for him. His chin crashes into my shoulder as he grabs hold of my arms. Then he starts slipping toward the ground, and for a minute, I think we're both going to fall down. I yank him up from under his arms, and he grabs hold of me like we're practically hugging, and I drag him into the house. I brace myself with my back foot so I can get my balance, and then lean Jake up against the wall. I let go for a second, and he starts slipping toward the floor, knocking my mom's flower wreath off the wall.

I try to get a good look at his face, thinking he'll laugh, like knocking the wreath on the floor is the funniest thing in the world. But he doesn't laugh; he doesn't say anything. He doesn't even notice. Because he's there but not really *there*. And you can tell from the look in his eyes, he's not coming back soon, either.

By the time our mom gets home, Jake's in bed and—in between getting up and putting my hand under his nose to make sure he's still breathing—I'm lying in my bunk looking at the Stargell. My mom comes in and kisses me on the head, then stretches up on her toes to check on Jake.

The car alarm starts blaring in my head. I want to tell her everything: about Jake not trying out for base-ball, about driving around with Andy Timmons and almost getting killed by a bread truck, and about Mr. Miller and Coach Gillis saying things that make it sound like even they know what's going on.

Instead, I say that Jake wasn't feeling too good.

She puts her hand on his forehead, says "Hmmm," then turns out the light and leaves.

The next morning after breakfast, I see Jake in the bathroom squirting Visine in his eyes. He blinks in my general direction a couple of times and I stop in the hall like I have something important to say. Something about last night, like how I'm not gonna cover up for him anymore. But he looks like he feels so rotten, that I can't.

"Wanna come to my game this afternoon?" I say.

He just stares at me.

"It's a home game," I say.

He shakes his head. "I don't think so, Toby."

He walks past, socks me in the arm, and then calls out to me from our room. "Here," he says. "Wear this for luck."

He throws me his lucky baseball jersey from the division championships. Even though I'm a total sucker for that sort of sentimental baseball stuff, it doesn't make me feel at all elated or even grateful. But I still say thanks.

I wear the jersey that day. Not because I'm the Miss Manners of baseball or anything, but because I figure it might be bad luck not to. Which means I have to wait around while the assistant-assistant coach scribbles out my old number on the clipboard and everyone else goes out on the field to warm up, which means I have a minute to check the stands and see if maybe Jake came after all.

Which is when I see Andy Timmons's car screeching through the parking lot, with Jake in the driver's seat. Jake, who doesn't even have a license. He swerves, then slams on the brakes, just barely missing a bunch of chess geeks. One kid spills all his chess pieces on the pavement. Jake yells something at him, then he speeds off, and I trudge out to Outer Mongolia trying to look like I didn't see what everybody just saw.

I sit on the bench for the whole game until the bottom of the eighth, when Sean, the usual catcher, keeps messing up and Coach Gillis subs me in. I put the catcher's gear on in a hurry, wondering if a person having a heart attack at age thirteen would set some kind of Guinness World Record. I snap the face mask down and pray that Jake's jersey brings me luck after all.

The first pitch rolls between my legs. The second one sails over my head. And the third one pops out of my glove. I scrabble around in the dirt on my hands and knees, trying to find the ball and wishing for an earthquake or at least a hailstorm or some other act of God to put me out of my misery. Then when I finally find it, I throw it back to the pitcher, winging it so far off to his right that the shortstop has to toss it back to him.

I get back into position and prepare to die a long,

agonizing death of embarrassment. Then the ball is whizzing toward me again. There's a tinny sound as the batter smacks the ball. I can see the ball arcing off into the air directly overhead. I throw my mask off, take a step forward, then a step back, then make a dive for it. I end up on my knees in a cloud of dust, staring at the ball in my mitt and wondering if I'm having a stress-induced hallucination.

But people seem to be cheering. Then I see the batter kick the dust and walk back to the bench. I still don't move, though, until the ump comes over and tells me that I need to throw the ball back to the pitcher so we can continue the game. At which point I wonder if a person can die of relief.

Which I don't. I just catch. I don't drop the ball, I don't miss it, I just catch, like I'm in a zone where it's just me and the pitcher playing catch. And then the inning's somehow over.

Before I can even recover from my near-death catching experience, I'm up at bat. I take a swing at the first pitch and then watch it cross the plate while my bat slices through the empty air. I swear not to do that again. Then I do it again. The pitcher winds up again and the ball comes hurtling toward me. Then I'm watching the bat connect, then watching the ball fly back across the field, then watching my legs pump as I run toward first. In my peripheral vision, I also see the shortstop miss the ball, and I keep running, rounding first, then taking second. When it's all over, I'm standing there panting and thinking that if I do die, at least the school paper will say that it was after I got a hit.

The next two batters strike out and Badowski hits a pop fly, so the game is over and my double didn't really count for anything. But at least Coach Gillis comes up and gives me a "good game" smack on the back.

Then he sort of does a double take at my jersey, like he's just realizing that it's the one he let Jake keep after last year's championships. He shakes his head and walks away.

On the bus on the way home, I'm sitting there wondering how a person can have a good game and still feel so rotten, when Arthur reaches over and gives me a Little Debbie.

"Good game," he says, nudging me in the ribs.

I just nod.

He tugs on my jersey.

"Is this Jake's old jersey?"

I sort of nod.

"What's with your brother, anyhow?"

"What do you mean, what's *with* him?" I say.

"I don't know," Arthur says. "*You're* his brother."

I shrug.

"I heard he got in-house suspension for cutting class," he says.

"I know," I say, even though up till now I didn't.

"He hangs out with Andy Timmons all the time now."

"So?"

"He's different. That's all."

"So?"

Arthur looks at me like I'm dangerous or something. Like all of a sudden I might go postal, which makes me *feel* sort of like I might go postal—which is not something I want to do, especially to the person who gives me his Little Debbies every day and who's been my best friend since fourth grade.

But which doesn't mean he's the kind of person you can talk to about things like your brother turning into someone who comes in at 1:16 all the time. Or about your mom turning into someone who doesn't notice, because she's always on a date with the Food King. Or about how you've turned into someone who's always lying and covering up about your brother coming in at

1:16. And about how you wonder if what you're doing is making things better, or just making them worse.

At which point I give him back the Little Debbie and tell him I'm not really hungry after all.

That night after dinner, I kick Jake's chair when I get up to put my plate in the dishwasher.

"What's your problem?" he says.

Normally, when one person says "What's your problem?" the other one says *"You're* my problem." After that, either person has the right to punch, head-lock, or pinch the other one, which pretty much always leads to a full-fledged wrestling match. Which pretty much always makes both people feel better.

"You're my problem," I say.

I wait for him to punch, headlock, or pinch me. But he just stares at me.

"So deal with it," he says.

Which I do. I get up from the table, go upstairs, open his dresser, and pull out the plastic bag. Then I walk into the bathroom, turn the bag upside down, and dump everything in the toilet. I flush twice just to be safe. I'm back at the table in time for dessert.

Later, after our mom leaves on another date with the Food King, Jake comes in our room and starts rummaging through his bottom drawer.

"It's not there." I say this like it's something that just happened, not something I had anything to do with.

He gets down on his hands and knees like a dog and throws everything out of the drawer. Then he smiles at me like he figures I'm playing a joke on him. "Okay, Toby," he says. "Where is it?"

I smack my lips and rub my belly.

"Seriously," he says. "Where is it?"

I put my hand on the doorknob.

"I threw it away," I say.

"Are you serious?"

I don't say yes or no. Which means yes.

I start to walk out. Then I turn around and look at him.

"What're you gonna do?" I say. "Tell Mom?"

After which I go downstairs and turn on the TV. A couple of minutes later, I hear the front door close. I look out the window and see Jake running across the parking lot.

So I do the only other thing a person can do at a

time like this. I go upstairs and pull my card collection down from the shelf and open it up to the page where the Stargell is. Usually it sort of falls open to that page because I look at it so much.

Except that it isn't there.

Bill Matlock is there and Tim Foli and Phil Garner and the other guys from the '79 World Series team, but right in the middle, where Willie Stargell's hopeful young rookie face is supposed to be, is blank.

I flip back and forth thinking maybe I accidentally moved it, but I know, the way you just know some things, that it's gone.

A fast-moving sweat spreads all over me, like when you go from cold to hot in a split second right before you throw up. But I don't throw up.

I just sit there and stare at the not-there-ness of the Stargell.

I don't know how long I've been staring at the empty page, when Eli comes in and taps me on the shoulder.

"Toby," he says. "Mr. Furry's missing again."

I don't say anything.

"What if he went over to the highway?"

"So?"

"So, it's a death trap."

All at once I feel as mean and rotten and hateful as a person can feel. "So," I say, "maybe he'll get killed."

Eli's mouth drops open. He takes a step back from me. Then he runs out of the room.

I still don't move. I feel like I'm standing far away from my actual self—watching myself be mean and rotten and hateful and not even caring that I don't care. Finally, after a long time, I get up and go downstairs. I don't know what I'm expecting exactly. I just go downstairs. I look around for Eli but there's no sign of him. I go in the kitchen, wander around, then go back to the den and flop down on the couch.

I wait for Eli to come in and fight over the remote. But he doesn't.

"Eli?" I call out.

There's no answer.

I get up and look around to see if he's hiding behind a chair or under the kitchen table like he does sometimes. But he's not there.

I call out his name again and then notice his yellow blankie on the floor next to the front door. My mind registers this as weird, but I keep calling out for him. Until I look out the window and see that Tonto is missing.

That's when my mouth goes dry, and my heart starts pounding, and I understand that he's gone.

I fling open the door and yell out his name. I don't even stop and wait for him to answer because I know he's not going to. Because I know where he is. He's over at the highway looking for his cat.

I take off running harder than I've ever run in my whole life, willing my feet and legs to fly. But it feels like I'm hardly moving. Somehow I'm winded before I even get to the end of the parking lot. I decide not to think about this, to just concentrate on putting one foot down, then the next, then the next, praying that if I just keep doing the same thing over and over that I'll arrive at wherever Eli is and everything will be okay.

Finally, after what feels like forever, I'm running alongside the highway. I'm on a skinny strip of grass that has a ditch full of weeds on one side and cars and trucks going by so close on the other side that I think that any minute, I'm going to be sucked into the undertow of a big truck and pulled out onto the road. I don't even dare to look up. I just keep my eyes down, watching the bits of trash and soda cans pass by underfoot.

Then I see something that looks familiar: a bag of Liver Lovin' cat treats spilled all over the grass. I stop and look up, then down the grassy strip. I force myself to call out Eli's name.

But there's no answer. I don't understand. I don't see how there can be absolutely no sign of him—no bike, no cowboy hat—nothing except a stupid bag of cat treats. I yell his name over and over and over until I'm crying, really truly crying like a baby.

When I get home, there's a police car in front of our apartment and all the lights are on. I stand there, frozen, in the parking lot. It's quiet, way too quiet. Then the police radio crackles to life. An angry voice barks out some numbers and codes and things that sound important and urgent, but which don't say anything about whether a person's little brother is okay or not. Then the radio goes dead.

I take a step toward our apartment, then stop. I take another step, planning to just keep going until I get to the front door. But I can't. Instead, I walk toward the police car. I circle it slowly, noticing that the trunk is partway open, and then edge my way toward the back. Which is when I see Tonto lying in the trunk.

I break into a run, slipping on the grass as I try to get traction. I have no any idea where I'm going. I just know I have to get out of there. But just as I regain my balance and start to cross the yard, another police car pulls up. I duck around the corner and hide behind the Dumpster.

A big, angry-looking police officer gets out of the car, checks the address, then walks to our door and disappears inside. I wait and wait, but nothing happens. My teeth are chattering even though it's not cold. I clench my jaw to stop the chattering. Then I start to shiver. I wrap my arms around my chest and try to make the shivering stop.

And then I hear a sound from under the Dumpster. First, there's a rustling noise. And then, clear as can be, comes a meow. When I kneel down and look underneath, I'm face-to-face with Mr. Furry. Her eyes are wide and shiny and she looks terrified, even more terrified than I am.

I pick her up. Gently. And she doesn't resist. Without even thinking, I walk back across the yard, carrying her like a baby until we get to the front door. Then I stand there a minute trying to figure out how to open the door without disturbing Mr. Furry. I swallow, push the doorbell with my elbow, and wonder what I'll see when the door opens.

What I see is Eli sitting on the couch, his blankie wrapped around his shoulders, an ice pack on his head.

The angry-looking police officer holds the door open. A lady police officer is sitting in a chair holding a notebook, and my mom is on the couch blowing her nose into a paper towel.

When Eli sees me, he jumps off the couch, grabs Mr. Furry out of my arms, and puts her in a headlock. He kisses her and nuzzles his nose in her fur, and scolds her and says he thought she was dead, and then kisses her some more. And I stand there with nothing in my arms, trying to believe what I'm seeing, and thinking that if Eli were a cat or a dog or some other kind of pet, I'd kiss him and nuzzle him and scold him and tell him I thought he was dead, and then kiss him some more.

Instead, I reach out toward the bump on his head.

"Does it hurt?" The words come out shaky.

He looks up at me.

"Nah," he says, wrapping his blankie around Mr. Furry. "It's okay."

All of a sudden I'm really, really tired. All I want to do is sit down on the couch and not move for about 185 years. Except that there are two police officers with actual guns and holsters in our house.

"Like I was saying," the big, angry-looking one says

to my mom. "He's a lucky boy. One inch in the other direction . . ."

My mom holds up her hand to make him stop.

Eli looks up at me again. "I fell off my bike. Right next to the highway." He says this sort of proudly.

I look at my mom.

She buries her face in the paper towel.

"Lucky for Eli," the officer says to me, "he fell into the weeds." He gestures toward the lady officer. "Officer Rodriguez, here, came by a minute later and found him standing on the side of the highway, crying."

Eli yawns. "I'm going to put Mr. Furry to bed," he says. "She's probably tired after her ordeal." Then he slings the cat over his shoulder and leaves.

For a minute, I think I might laugh. For just a second, it seems so ridiculous and also so ridiculously normal that Eli's tucking Mr. Furry in for the night, wrapped in his blankie, using words like "ordeal." I think I might laugh the way Eli does, that I might fall on the floor and laugh until I can't breathe.

Until I see the angry-looking officer giving me a suspicious look. I bite the inside of my mouth.

"What we're concerned about now . . ." he says, once Eli is gone, "is your other brother."

My stomach drops.

"Did something happen to Jake?" I say.

No one says anything.

"Is he okay?"

My mom puts her hands up to her face like she's praying. The lady officer shifts in her seat and her holster makes a creaking sound. The angry-looking officer clears his throat but he doesn't say anything.

"What?" My voice practically cracks in half. "What's going on?"

I look over at my mom. Her eyes are red and puffy, and she looks pale and tired and small. She just shakes her head.

The angry-looking officer explains. "While Officer Rodriguez was out with your little brother in the back of her cruiser, I had your big brother in the back of mine."

All I can do is nod.

"He was playing a game where he drove his friend's car back and forth from one lane to the other. Out on Creekside Road."

I swallow.

"Ran off the road, sideswiped a parked car, took out a couple of mailboxes."

I hold my breath and wait for him to say that Jake's in the hospital, that he's in a coma, that he's dead.

"No serious injuries," he says matter-of-factly. "Just property damage."

I slump back against the wall and exhale.

The police officer studies me, like he's waiting for me to say something. Officer Rodriguez has her pen poised over her notebook.

I look at them, then over at my mom. Then I tug on the brim of my baseball cap and pull it down as far as it will go.

The angry-looking officer sighs. Then he says my mom's name.

"I'm sorry to have to tell you this, ma'am," he says, not actually sounding very sorry. "It appears they were under the influence."

"They were drinking?" my mom says.

"Well, yes, we found beer in the car, and a pint of bourbon," he says. "We'll have to wait till the tests come back. But it also appears that they'd been using other substances."

I peek out from under my hat and see my mom put her hand up to her mouth. "Drugs?"

He nods.

"Jake?"

"Yes, ma'am."

She looks at me.

I look down at my shoes.

When I look up a minute later, she's crying, and Officer Rodriguez is patting her on the shoulder.

Then the angry-looking officer says she needs to come down to the police station, and that the juvenile-court judge is on his way in. "In situations like these, the judge usually has them detox at Mount Tom for a couple of days before he convenes the case," he says.

My mom flinches at the word *detox*.

But she gets up and puts on her coat. She stuffs her wadded-up paper towel in her pocket and starts to leave. Then she stops, goes into the kitchen, and comes back with a pack of cigarettes. The next thing I know, all the adults are gone, and I'm standing there by myself in the den, wondering if what just happened really happened.

It's almost two o'clock and I'm lying in bed listening to Eli and Mr. Furry breathe, when the front door opens. I strain to hear if there are two sets of footsteps or one.

One person comes up the steps, slowly. The door to my mom's room opens, then shuts. And I lie there, picturing myself going over and knocking on the door and patting her on the shoulder like Officer Rodriguez did, until finally, around three A.M., the crying stops.

Even though it's a school day, it's practically eleven o'clock by the time I wake up the next day. Eli's bed is empty. I get up and check Jake's bed, even though I know it's empty. I knock on my mom's door. When she doesn't answer I open it a crack.

Her room is dark like a cave and smells like cigarettes.

"Mom?"

There's some rustling from the bed. "What time is it?" she says.

I tell her it's almost eleven.

She doesn't say anything back, so I close the door and go downstairs.

Eli's on the couch eating Pringles, watching Cartoon Network, and holding Mr. Furry in a death grip.

I sit down next to him and don't say anything. I'm not actually watching TV, though. I'm sitting there looking straight ahead, trying to get up the nerve to fully look at Eli to see if he really is okay.

Something funny happens on the show. Eli practically has a conniption laughing. Mr. Furry uses the opportunity to escape. I use the opportunity to look over at Eli. He's got a purplish bump on his forehead. When I see it, my chest hurts—actually, physically hurts.

I jump up and go in the kitchen. Then I just stand there looking around for something to make the feeling in my chest go away. Finally, after it doesn't, I reach in the refrigerator and grab a couple of sodas.

Eli looks sort of surprised when I come back and hand him a soda.

"Are you sure this is okay?"

Technically, it's not okay, since we're not allowed to have soda in the morning. "Yeah," I say. "It's definitely okay."

Eli just looks at the soda can. Then he looks at me. "You don't have to give me a soda just because of last night," he says.

I don't quite know what to say. So I pull the pop-top on his soda and hand it to him. Which is not the same as saying I'm sorry and that I'm glad he's okay, but which is at least something.

W e sit there watching cartoons for a long time, not saying anything.

Finally, Eli taps me on the shoulder.

"What's going on, anyhow?"

"What do you mean?"

"Where's Jake?"

I try to sound casual. "I don't know."

"How come mom's still asleep and we get to stay home on a school day watching cartoons?"

I try to think of a little-kid explanation, something that's true but that isn't the whole truth, either. Something that doesn't let on that Jake is in a place called Mount Tom, detoxing. Something that doesn't let on that things with Mom might be bad again. Something that won't worry a kid who almost lost his cat and could've gotten killed on the highway last night.

"It's a day off."

Eli just looks at me.

"You know how some kids get to take off on random days for Hanukkah or Kwanzaa or something that not everybody else gets to take off for?"

He nods.

"It's sort of like that."

It's the middle of the afternoon and we're still watching Cartoon Network and our mom is still in her room with the door closed when the phone rings. Eli gets it.

"I'll go check," he says to the person on the phone. Then he goes up to our mom's room.

A little while later, he comes back and picks up the receiver. "She says she can't come to the phone," he says.

He says "Okay, okay" to whoever's on the phone, then hangs up and comes back into the den.

"Who was that?"

"Stanley."

"His Heinie?"

"He says we can call him Stanley."

I look over and notice that Eli is wearing his Pokey Reese T-shirt.

He notices me noticing the T-shirt.

"He's not that bad, Toby," Eli says.

I get up, turn the Implosion picture faceup, and head out the front door.

Eli looks worried. "Where are you going?" he says.

"I have to go do something," I say, not having any idea what that something is, just knowing that I can't sit there anymore watching cartoons and pretending it's a day off.

"Who's taking care of me?"

I don't quite know what to say. So I go in the kitchen where Mr. Furry is taking a nap in a patch of sun, pick her up, and carry her out to the couch.

Mr. Furry gives me an annoyed look, but Eli seems content.

"I'll be back," I say.

Tonto's lying in the front yard, so I grab him and start riding, not knowing exactly where I'm going. I ride around for a while, watching the pavement go by under the front wheel. I ride out of our apartment complex, up to the overpass and down the other side. I keep riding and riding, until I'm practically right in front of Mr. D's.

Which is about the last place in the universe I can go now that the Stargell is gone.

I slam on the brakes, turn around, and peel out. I pump old Tonto like a madman till I get to the end of Mr. D's block. Then I take a quick look back over my shoulder to see if Mr. D's standing in the middle of his driveway wondering whose tires were squealing in front of his house.

Which he's not.

Which is a relief, sort of, but which is also, to tell you the truth, more of a letdown.

After a while, I get back on the bike and ride up to the overpass. I sit there on Tonto, letting the wind from the trucks blow my sweatshirt around for a while, then I start riding again, slowly, like I'm just going to keep riding and riding until I'm somewhere like Ohio or Omaha.

Or California.

I put on a burst of speed and head for the Mini Mart. When I get there I'm practically out of breath, but the woman at the counter, who has big hair and big nails, doesn't even look at me; she just glances up at the security screen TV in front of her, then goes back to her word search. I walk to the back of the store, near the restrooms, to the pay phone.

I dial the operator and tell her I need the number for Thomas Malone in California.

"L.A.?" she says.

"Pardon me?"

"In Los Angeles?" she says.

I say I guess so and she gives me another number to call, saying another operator will assist me. But the other operator doesn't really seem too interested in assisting me; she sounds like she's in a room with about 400 other operators who are in too big a hurry taking care of real calls to bother with me.

"Would you like the Thomas Malone on El Paso?"

I say okay. I feed about 185 coins into the slot and

then get one of those prerecorded answering-machine robot voices, which doesn't say I've reached the home of Tom Malone or anything personal like that. It just says, "Please. Leave. A. Message."

I'm not ready when the beep sounds. "Dad?" I clear my throat. "If this is you, could you please call us back? Something bad happened and Jake's in trouble and Mom needs money." I know instantly that mentioning money is a mistake. "Not a lot, probably," I say, swallowing. "Anyhow, that's it. I, um, hope you're having a good time, you know, in California." Then, like he's somebody who doesn't even know us, I read off our phone number nice and slow.

I get back on Tonto and ride up to the overpass. I stop and look at all the cars whooshing by underneath and try not to look like a juvenile delinquent riding a little kid's bike around in the middle of a school day. Instead, I try to look like it's no big deal that I'm standing on the overpass in the middle of a school day. Like maybe I'm a kid who's home-schooled and who's just hanging out trying to do a word problem in my head, like figuring out how many hours it takes for someone driving a Jeep 65 miles an hour nonstop to get from California to Pittsburgh.

When I get home Eli's still on the couch watching cartoons.

I sit down next to him. "Anybody call?" I ask him.

He doesn't answer.

"Eli. Did anybody call?"

"For you?" he says.

"Not just for me," I say. "Just in general."

He shrugs.

"You know, anybody special?" I say.

Eli gives me a look. "You mean Stanley?"

"No, not him," I say.

Eli doesn't answer; he just goes back to watching his show.

"I'm hungry," he says.

"So get some cereal," I say.

"There's no milk."

I sigh, then get up, thinking that even a bunch of Food King appetizers would taste good right about now. Except that there aren't any left. The only thing I can find is a pack of microwave popcorn, which I'm nuking when the phone rings.

I practically run across the room to get it. Then I stand there and let it ring one more time so it doesn't sound like I'm all out of breath when I pick up.

"Is Suzy there?" It's a man's voice, a sort of familiar man's voice, which I figure could be my dad's new California voice or could be him feeling sort of shy and polite after having not called for so long.

I decide to also be polite.

"May I ask who's calling?" I say.

"Stanley."

It takes me a minute to understand. "The Food King?" I say.

He chuckles. "My friends call me Stanley."

I don't say anything.

Finally, he says, "Is your mom there?"

I could go up and try to wake her up. I could cover the phone with my hand and pretend to call for her. Instead, I say she can't come to the phone.

"Oh." You can hear him sounding kind of concerned, also kind of stumped. He stays on the phone, breathing, for a minute.

I hold my breath.

"Is this Toby?" he says.

I nod.

"Will you let her know I called, Toby?"

I say uh-huh, which isn't the same as saying yes; then the microwave bell rings, and I tell him I have to go.

The next day, it's the same. Eli and I sit on the couch pretending it's another day off and eating cereal out of the box. About lunchtime, the phone rings. I practically vault over Mr. Furry, who's back to napping in the kitchen.

"Is this Toby?" The connection is scratchy, but it's definitely a man's voice and he's asking for me.

I swallow. "Uh-huh," I say. "This is Toby."

"I got your call," the voice says.

I get ready to explain everything.

"By mistake," he says.

I don't understand.

"Did you leave an answering machine message saying someone named Jake was in trouble?"

I nod.

"I'm sorry," he says. "But I think you dialed the wrong number." He sounds like he actually *is* sorry.

"It's okay," I say. Even though it's not okay at all.

Then we stay on the phone, not saying anything for a while.

He wishes me good luck.

"Good-bye, Toby," he says, like we actually know each other, which makes me wish there were a reason to stay on the phone with him. But I can't think of one, so I just hang up.

"Who was that?" says Eli when I come back into the den.

I shrug. "Just some guy."

I go upstairs and, just to make myself feel completely rotten, open my binder and look at the not there-ness of the Stargell. Then I get in bed and pull the covers over my head, even though I'm still dressed, and lie there for about 185 years.

I wait for it to feel warm and soft and dark like it does under Eli's blankie. Which doesn't happen. Then I wait for my mom to wake up and notice that I'm in bed with the covers over my head. Which also doesn't happen. Then I wait and wait and hope that if I just wait long enough that maybe someday I'll feel like I used to feel when I looked at the Stargell. Which is never going to happen.

I finally throw the covers back and get up. And go outside and get back on Tonto. This time, knowing that where I need to go isn't Ohio or Omaha.

Mr. D doesn't throw me any WarHeads when I walk in or ask me how I'm doing. "I don't have any jobs for you today," is all he says.

"That's okay," I say.

He goes back to looking at his computer screen,

which I can see is showing a Milt May rookie card for sale on eBay.

"There's a Milt May for sale," he says. Which is probably just something to say, since I already have a Milt May, which he sold me back in sixth grade. I feel like all of a sudden I'm just another customer and not the one person in the world he gave a mint '62 Stargell rookie card.

I don't tell him I'm done collecting cards. I don't tell him there's no point. "I'll think about it."

Mr. D just looks at me.

"There's something I have to tell you," I say.

He reaches over to log off, and the computer voice says good-bye.

Mr. D tugs at the hem of his Mister Rogers sweater. I run my hand through my hair and stare at the toes of my shoes. "The, uh, you know, the Stargell . . ." I say.

He nods.

I'm sweating to death, my mouth is dry, and my heart is pounding. For once in my hypochondriac life, I truly do feel sick. I can't finish.

I peek out from under the brim of my baseball cap and look at Mr. D. He looks like maybe he feels sick, too.

Which makes me feel even worse.

After a while, Mr. D clears his throat. "You don't have it anymore, do you?" he says.

I shake my head no. And wonder how he always knows things without me telling him.

"I saw it on the Internet," he says.

I nod.

He waits a while. "Is that because you sold it, Toby?"

I want to explain everything.

But I just keep my eyes down and say no.

"I didn't think so," he says.

I look up at him for a minute. "You didn't?"

He shakes his head. "But I did wonder why you weren't coming around."

I shrug.

"Are you mad at me?" I say finally.

"Mad? No."

When you ask grown-ups if they're mad and they say, no, they're not mad, they usually say they're disappointed, which, to tell you the truth, is a lot worse.

"Are you disappointed?" I say.

"Why would I be disappointed?"

I shrug. "Because I lost it?"

He waits a minute. "Did you?" he says. "Did you lose it?"

I know this is one of those Yoda–Luke Skywalker situations where he keeps answering my questions with more questions until I finally understand what he's talking about, but all I say is no.

"All right, then," he says. He gets up, goes behind the counter, and then tosses me a pack of WarHeads.

Which means I have to look right at him. "Thanks," I say, meaning not just for the WarHeads.

He nods. "It's okay," he says, also, I'm pretty sure, meaning not just about the WarHeads.

I don't know what to do after that, so I grab the Windex and walk over to the display case, partly out of habit, partly because it's at least something to do.

Mr. D turns his computer back on.

After a while he says my name.

"You see the new Jason Kendall in there?" he says. He gets up and comes over with the key to open the case. "Wanna spend a little quality time with it?"

"No thanks," I say.

He studies me a minute. "You finished collecting?"

"Maybe," I say. Then I go back to Windexing the display case.

"Does the Stargell have anything to do with that?" he says.

"Maybe," I say again.

He frowns.

I want him to understand. Even though I'm not sure I understand myself. I look him in the eye and decide to tell him the best I can.

"I don't ever want to have something be that important again."

He looks like he understands. "Because it might disappear on you?"

I nod.

"So from now on you're going to avoid caring about things," he says. "That way you're never disappointed, right?" he says.

"I guess so," I say.

"Well, *that*," he says. "*That* would disappoint me."

When I get home, Eli's still sitting there watching TV, which is either some kind of Guinness World Record or which means he's getting that psychological disease when people are afraid to go outside and end up spending the rest of their lives sitting on their couch.

He hardly even looks away from the screen when I come in. "I'm hungry," he says.

I go in the kitchen and look around. I come back with a jar of peanut butter and two spoons, since that's all that's left. And even though I'm pretty hungry on account of having not eaten anything all day except WarHeads, I let him have more than me.

We're sitting there with the empty jar between us when my mom comes down wearing her bathrobe. Her eyes are puffy, and she looks really tired even though she's been asleep for two days.

She doesn't say anything right away. She just looks around the den at the empty cereal boxes and the empty bag of popcorn and the empty box of PopTarts.

I jump off the couch and start cleaning up.

"Is that what you had for dinner?" She points to the peanut butter jar.

Eli nods.

"It's okay, Mom," I say.

She puts her hand on my shoulder and I sit back down.

"No." She shakes her head like she's privately agreeing with herself about something. "It's not okay."

She gets up and goes into the kitchen and makes us a meal out of a whole bunch of canned things and frozen things, which don't really go together but are at least cooked things, and Eli and I eat like people who just got off a starvation diet. She doesn't eat any of the food, though; she just looks out the window.

After dinner, while Eli's gone off to play Nintendo and I'm telling her how great dinner was for the 185th time, she starts flipping through the mail. She holds up a copy of *Sports Illustrated* with a banner across the front thanking me for my new subscription.

"You can forget about baseball cards for a while, Toby," she says. "Until you pay for this."

I just say okay.

Then she holds up a copy of *Cooking Lite*. "I assume you ordered this, too."

I nod.

"Why?" she says.

"I dunno," I say.

"Answer me, Toby," she says.

I look down at my feet, then up at the cover of *Cooking Lite*, which has a picture of homemade apple pie on the cover and a headline that says, *Surprise your family tonight!*

"I did it so we could win the million dollars," I say.

She sighs.

And I just stand there waiting for her to start crying.

Except that she doesn't. Not only does she not start crying, she starts laughing. Not in the usual way, but in a way that you can tell she doesn't think this is one bit funny. Which, to tell, you the truth, is way worse than her looking like she has a rare, incurable disease.

She puts her hands on her hips and stares at me.

"Do you want to tell me what's been going on around here?"

I can tell from the way she's saying it, that she expects me to shrug or say I don't know. Or maybe come up with another one of my bogus stories.

But I say yes.

"Yes," I say again. "I do."

At which point, I realize it's the first truly true thing I've said to her in a long time.

She pulls a cigarette out of her robe pocket, looks at it, then puts it back. She gestures for me to sit down at the kitchen table.

She waits for me to say something.

I also wait for me to say something.

"Jake, uh . . ." I swallow. "Jake's not on the baseball team."

She waits for me to say more.

I wait for me to say more, too, but I can't.

She squints at me. She takes out a cigarette and lights it this time. She looks sideways at me as she's blowing out the match.

"You knew, didn't you?" she says.

I shrug the kind of shrug where you say yes without technically saying yes.

"And you covered up for him?"

I pick up a coupon that fell out of the copy of *Cooking Lite* and fold it in half. I nod.

"Why?" she says.

I fold the coupon in half again. "I was just trying to help."

"You were trying to help?" she says, blowing out a plume of smoke.

I nod.

She just waits.

"I thought you'd get upset." I fold the coupon in half again, then again, then again. Finally, I look up at her. "I didn't think you could handle it."

She gets up and goes over to the sink to flick the ashes off her cigarette.

"Besides," I say to her back, "you were always on the phone with *him*."

She turns around and I point to the Food King box sticking out of the trash can.

"Stanley?"

"Whatever."

She takes a long inhale, then crushes her cigarette in

the sink. She paces around the kitchen a little, reties the belt of her robe, wipes down the counter. Then she grabs the carton of cigarettes, dumps them in the trash, and comes back and sits down at the table.

"I'm sorry," she says.

I don't understand. I'm the one who's supposed to be sorry. "About him?" I gesture toward the Food King box.

"No," she says. "About the whole thing."

I wonder exactly what she means by this.

"A person only sees what they want to see," she says.

I still don't understand. I only know that she's starting to sound like Mr. D.

She takes my chin in her hand. "I thought something was going on. I just didn't want it to be true."

I think about this for a minute. It occurs to me that I didn't want it to be true either, that I thought that maybe if I sprayed enough Citrus Magic around the house, it wouldn't technically, actually be true.

She reaches over and messes my hair. Then she stops and looks at me.

"Are you still pulling out your gray hair?"

"Not exactly," I say. "I rearrange it."

She fiddles with my hair, moving it around with professional, Hairport-style moves. She stands back and looks at me.

"Don't worry," she says.

Don't worry is the kind of thing people say all the time. But you can tell by the way she's saying it, she really means it, and she needs me to know she really means it.

So I say okay.

I think maybe we're done, but she scrunches up her eyebrows.

"Is there anything else you want to tell me?" she says.

I look the other way.

She waits.

"He took my Stargell."

I look back; her eyebrows are even more scrunched up. "What's a Stargell?" She says this like it's a word in a foreign language or a new rap group, like it's something she'll never understand.

It's the one card of the one player I cared about more than anyone in the world, the one guy who never left Pittsburgh for better money or better teams or better towns.

"It's just a baseball card," I say.

"Really?"

I look at her. Except that all of a sudden she's

blurry, because somehow my eyes are full of stupid, annoying tears. I look away and clear my throat. "Really."

She sighs. "You know, I think he stole from me, too," she says finally. "From the tip jar."

"I know," I say.

She nods, then she cups her hand over her mouth, like she just realized something. "I bet he took my pearl earrings, too," she says. "The ones your father gave me."

This is a major violation of the unspoken rule about not speaking about my dad. I fold the *Cooking Lite* coupon into about a million little squares and wait for her to say more.

She stares off into space, then blinks. "It's okay," she says. "I never liked them anyway."

I don't say anything.

"You know, he used to take money from the grocery envelope," she says. "For beer."

"Dad?" It's weird and also surprisingly not weird to finally say his name out loud.

She nods.

I hold my breath.

She pats the pocket of her robe, like she's looking for cigarettes. "I thought it was my job to take care of everything," she says. "I thought if I cleaned up after all the messes he made, then there wasn't a problem."

"I know," I say, because I really do know.

"I know you do," she says.

Then I get up and go over to the drawer next to the sink, where there's a pack of herbal stop-smoking gum the Food King bought for her. Which I toss her, underhand, slow-pitch style.

Right about then, Eli comes in carrying Mr. Furry in a choke hold. Which is not only amusing since Mr. Furry looks so miserable, but which also puts an end to my mom and me having an emotionally meaningful moment.

"Go clean up the den, you two," she says, popping some gum in her mouth. "I have some calls I have to make."

Out of habit, I start by going over to the Implosion picture. I dust it off with the elbow of my shirt and set it back down on top of the TV.

"Toby?" says Eli.

I turn around.

"He's not coming back, is he?"

"Who?"

Eli points to the Implosion picture. "Dad."

I stand there for about 185 years looking at Eli in

his blankie and cowboy hat, until I know what I'm going to say.

"I don't think so," I say finally.

As soon as I say it, I know it's true. Which, to tell you the truth, doesn't make me feel all emotionally out of control like it maybe it should. In fact, it feels surprisingly *not* weird, like maybe it was pretty much what I'd figured all along.

"It's okay, Toby," says Eli.

I don't get it.

"He's like the Easter Bunny."

I still don't get it.

Eli flicks the light switch.

"You can still believe in him."

When I walk into homeroom the next day, everybody stops talking. Which means they were probably talking about Jake. Which doesn't technically have anything to do with me, but apparently people think they have to shut up about around me.

I walk toward my desk. And trip over Badowski's backpack, which is somehow suddenly in the middle of the aisle.

"Jeez, man," he says real loud. "What's the matter with you? You on drugs or something?"

I get a mental image of me punching Badowski in the face but I just walk past him, sit down, and wish I was actually home-schooled.

At lunch, Arthur comes and sits down next to me and starts eating his hamburger without saying hello or anything.

I look at him sideways. And see that he's looking at me sideways.

"You want my Jell-O?" he says.

I don't, on account of Jell-O being made from gelatin, which I heard is made from horses' hooves, which can probably give you something like Mad Horse disease, but since we haven't technically spoken since the day in the bus when I almost went postal, I figure it's the least I can do.

"Thanks," I say, not exactly meaning for the Jell-O. He just looks at me. "I hate Jell-O," he says.

Then we sit there for about 185 years, with him openly hating Jell-O and me pretending not to.

"That was weird in PE the other day when we played that Colonial America thing," he says finally.

I don't want to say that it wasn't that weird, so I just nod.

"Didn't it gross you out?" he says.

Telling a person you'll eat their secondhand Jell-O when you think it may give you some rare undiscovered terminal disease is one thing. But telling a person that it grossed you out to hold another person's hand when you actually liked it is another thing.

"Not exactly," I say.

Arthur looks relieved. "Yeah," he says. "Me neither."

He takes another bite of his hamburger. "You think Chrissy Russo might talk to me if I talk to her?" he says.

I guess there are people who like people who like talking about dead people. "Sure," I say. "If you talk about Kurt Cobain."

Then we sit there for another 185 years.

"About your brother . . ." he says.

I stop chewing and wonder if talking about Jake is going to maybe make me feel postal again like it did the other day on the bus. Then I get ready to say I'm sorry, because I don't want to be like I was the other day on the bus.

And then Arthur says he's sorry.

"You're sorry?"

"Yeah," he says. "Sorry it happened."

At which point, I decide that maybe Arthur *is* the

kind of person you can talk to about things. Like how you can be worried about what's going to happen to your brother, and how you can also still feel like killing him for taking your most precious possession. And how you can wish your brother would come home, and also wish you never had to see him again.

Which I make a mental note to do.

As soon as I figure out which way I feel.

That afternoon on the bus, Martha MacDowell sits down right next to me. Even though there are about forty-five other places she could have sat, and even though I don't have any junk food like Arthur—who gets on, looks at us sitting together, and actually doesn't do or say anything emotionally out-there or highly embarrassing and just goes and sits down in the back.

I try to think of something witty to say, knowing that under the circumstances I'll probably be about as talkative as Kurt Cobain.

She flips her hair over her shoulder, giving off the clean laundry smell. Then she looks at me. "You don't mind if I sit here, do you?"

I say yes, which I realize too late sounds like I *do* mind. But I don't. Which means the right answer, grammatically speaking, is no. Which means I then say no.

She looks at me like maybe I have a split personality disorder.

So I say "Stay," which makes me sound like an instructor in a dog obedience class.

She gives me a sort of weird look, but she stays.

I wipe my hands on my jeans.

I clear my throat.

"Nice weather out there," I say. I actually point out the window, which at that moment I want to jump out of.

But she smiles. "I like spring," she says.

"I like it too," I say.

Then we sat there liking spring for about 185 years.

"I like how it smells," I say finally. "Like dirt and stuff."

She laughs. "Like dirt? That's such a boy thing to say."

I start hoping the bus will be rear-ended by a Mack truck, which would either put me out of my misery or at least give me a reason to accidentally hold her hand.

"You have gray hair," she says finally, which coming from her sounds like a simple fact, not like I'm a freak of nature.

"They're not all gray," I say. "Just thirty-two of them."

She bursts out laughing.

"You're funny," she says.

I say thanks, then sit there trying to be funny again. Except that not only can I not say anything funny, I can't say anything at all.

"Hey," says Martha finally. "At least you're not bald."

At which point I burst out laughing, which to tell you the truth, isn't something I've felt like doing much lately.

Then she says we're at her stop. While she's gathering up her books, I lean toward her in a totally unobvious way, trying to get another whiff of her clean laundry smell and pretty much deciding to rule out the home-schooling thing.

For the rest of the ride and all the way home from the bus stop I feel about as good as a person can probably feel without actually being on antidepressants.

Until I get home and sit down on the couch and the doorbell rings. It's the Food King standing at our front door with a couple bags of Chinese food.

"Mind if I come in?" he says in his polite, nice-guy way.

I don't say if I mind or not, but I let him come in. "My mom's not home yet," I say.

"I know," he says. "She's on her way with Eli."

I nod and try to make a face like I knew that already, even though we both know I didn't. Then I stand there trying not notice how good the food smells.

"Smells good, doesn't it?" he says.

I shrug like maybe it does or maybe it doesn't.

"Do you think we should set the table?" he says.

I say I guess so, and then pray that we don't have to have a male bonding moment trying to decide which side the forks go on or something. At which point Eli comes blasting in through the front door and hugs, actually hugs, the Food King. My mom comes in right behind him, but before I have to witness the possibility of my mother having actual physical contact with someone of the opposite sex, Mr. Furry shoots out the front door.

"I'll get him," I say, secretly thanking Mr. Furry for giving me a chance to escape.

After which, I stalk Mr. Furry around ye olde condo, shaking the can of Liver Lovin' cat treats and trying not to think about everybody inside eating Chinese food without me.

Finally, I spot her under a bush next door. I reach

out for her but she swipes a paw at me, scratching my wrist. Apparently, Mr. Furry's forgotten all about our tender moment under the Dumpster the other night.

I walk across the yard, deciding she is a lame pet after all. I crouch down next to the Dumpster and make you-can-trust-me sounds. Then, when all she does is hiss at me, I make a grab for her. She skitters to the other side of the Dumpster. I'm about to swear at her when I realize someone's watching me.

It's the Food King.

"How's it going?"

I shrug.

"I've heard you're pretty good at this, but I thought maybe you could use some help."

I shrug again.

The Food King points to the liver treats. "May I?"

I think about the Chinese food inside getting cold, and I hand him the can. He takes them out one by one and makes a trail of liver treats leading from the Dumpster to our front door.

Then we both wait for Mr. Furry to come out. Which she eventually does, twitching her whiskers and giving me a highly offended look. But she eats the treats one by one, looking like her usual dignified self, until finally she's back at the front door.

I open the door and Mr. Furry trots inside.

I just look at the Food King.

He sort of shrugs. "Cats," he says. "You have to make them think it was their idea."

Then Eli hugs me, and calls me a cat rustler, and the Food King doesn't say anything about him being the one who technically rustled Mr. Furry, and we all sit down to eat.

My mom asks Stanley if he'll take a look at the screen door before he leaves.

"It probably just needs a little WD40," he says.

My mom gets up to get soy sauce.

"Maybe sometime I'll come over with some grass seed, once it finally warms up," he calls out to her in the kitchen. "For that that spot out front where the bike left a bare patch."

"Tonto," says Eli.

"Beg your pardon?" says Stanley.

Eli climbs under the table to feed a noodle to Mr. Furry. Which means it's just me and Stanley.

"Tonto," I say. "The bike's named Tonto." I start out saying this with a totally straight face, but by the time I'm done, I'm smiling like ye olde village idiot.

But the Food King just smiles at me.

"Okay," he says. "Thanks for telling me that."

Then we just eat, and he helps clear the table. When my mom says she doesn't have any dessert, he says he's got to get going anyhow.

My mom walks the Food King to the front door. I position myself so I can see if they hug or anything without them seeing me watching. But she just thanks him for the Chinese food and then he's gone.

"Is he going to be our new dad?" Eli says this before the door is even totally closed.

My mom makes a face like this is a silly question.

"Stanley?" she says.

"I like him," says Eli, who then walks out holding Mr. Furry in a death grip.

Which just leaves me and my mom standing in the kitchen.

"So what's going on?" I say.

"With Stanley?"

I make a face like that's a silly question. "With Jake."

She motions for me to sit down at the table, then pulls out some of her herbal gum.

"The judge . . ." she says, ". . . gave him probation."

Probation at school means you have to sit in the principal's office during recess. I don't exactly understand what it means when a judge says it.

"When he comes back."

Now I really don't understand.

"Is the judge going away?"

"No." She puts her hand on mine. "Jake is."

"Where's he going?"

"Rehab."

All of sudden I feel as mean and rotten and hateful as I did the night he took the Stargell. I pull my hand away.

"Doesn't he have to go to jail?"

"No."

"Doesn't he have to pay anyone back?"

"You mean for the damage to the car and the mailboxes?"

I mean for the Stargell, too. "For everything."

She looks confused. "Why are you so angry?"

"I don't get it." I get up and turn my back to her.

"What don't you understand?"

I turn around. "Everything."

She sighs and gets up to throw out her gum. "Well, we get to spend a day with him tomorrow before he goes."

"Tomorrow?"

"Tomorrow."

I turn and stomp out, making as much noise as I possibly can pounding up the steps. Which is pretty stupid because I have absolutely no idea what to do once I get upstairs. Which I solve by grabbing a copy of Eli's new *National Geographic for Kids* and going into the bathroom and sitting on the fuzzy green thing on the toilet and where I stay until I'm sure my mom and Eli have gone to sleep.

The next day when I wake up, I smell bacon. I look at the clock and see that it's only ten o'clock, which is weird since my mom's never up this early on a Saturday. What's weirder is that our house smells like real food.

I come downstairs, still feeling mad, but also feeling embarrassed for how I acted last night. Especially when I see her mixing a bowl of scrambled eggs and all.

Until I see Jake sitting at the kitchen table. At which point all I feel is mad.

I don't say hello or even let on that I notice that he's there. "I'm going to Mr. D's," I say, purposely not looking at him.

"Not today," my mom says. "Jake's only here till dinner, and I want everyone home."

I mentally try to figure out exactly how many minutes there are between now and six o'clock.

"Want some bacon and eggs?" she says.

"Nah," I say. I walk past Jake toward the pantry to get some cereal. Except that there isn't any. Which means I have to have eggs. "Okay," I say. "I guess I'll have some."

I sit down, purposely not sitting next to Jake like I usually do. Which means I'm sitting right across from him. Which means I pretty much have to look at him. His face looks banged up and he looks smaller than he used to, smaller and pale and tired, and not exactly like the person I felt like killing.

At which point Eli comes running in and practically tackles Jake. "You're back!" he says. He wraps his blankie around Jake's shoulders and Jake smiles. His lip is cracked. He touches it with his finger, like he just remembered it hurts to smile.

Then my mom brings over the food and asks Jake what he wants to do today.

He shrugs. "Play some Nintendo," he says, looking at Eli. "Maybe watch the Pirates game." I make a big deal out of chewing my bacon and looking at my plate so I don't have to see if maybe he looked at me when he said that.

Then breakfast is over, and Eli and Jake go up to play Nintendo while I stay in the kitchen, trying to figure out how exactly I'm going to spend the 428 minutes between now and dinner.

My mom is chewing her herbal stop-smoking gum and putting the dishes in the dishwasher.

"Aren't you mad at him?" I just blurt it out then wait for her to get mad. At me.

She closes the dishwasher. "Of course I am."

"Then why don't you act like it?"

"First of all, you don't know what I've said to Jake privately."

I consider this, but decide that she could still act mad instead of acting like he's company.

"And secondly," she says. "Being angry isn't going to help right now."

Which is something I definitely don't agree with, since being mad is about the only way I'm going to get through the next 427 minutes.

I'm sitting on the couch watching the Saturday afternoon pregame show—having killed 218 minutes reading the sports section, oiling my glove, going online, actually doing my homework, even skipping lunch just to avoid being in the same room with Jake—when I hear Mr. Furry meowing her head off at the back door.

Jake and Eli are upstairs playing Nintendo and my mom is in her room on the phone, so I get up, grab the liver treats, and open the door. Mr. Furry gives me a suspicious look. I reach down to show her I have a liver treat in my hand, but she obviously thinks I'm going to ambush her again.

At which point I decide to use the Food King technique. I make a trail of liver treats, leading from the bush to the door, not making any eye contact with her, which I figure is important for her cat dignity. I extend the trail all the way to the couch, and then go in and sit there oiling my glove, until a few minutes later, when she comes in and jumps up on the couch.

She gives me one of her aloof cat looks, which I realize is her way of saying that I'm sitting in her spot. I move over and the next thing I know, she's nudging her head into my palm for me to pet her. Which I do.

Her fur is surprisingly warm and soft. She stretches her neck out, clearly wanting me to scratch her. Which I do. At which point she starts to purr. And so I sit there, thinking that even though she's no Harriet the Horrible, she's at least someone who's small and soft and needing human attention, and who may possibly not be so lame after all.

Which means I'm sitting on the couch telling Mr.

Furry to watch how Brian Giles swings, when Jake comes in. It's more like I feel him come in, since I don't look up. Even when he sits down at the other end of the couch. Mr. Furry looks up and stretches, but then she just circles around in my lap, pushes her head up into my hand, and sits back down. After which I sit there trying not to move or not to even breathe, like the entire future of the free world depends on Mr. Furry not waking up and going over to sit with Jake.

Jake and I sit there watching the Pirates suck. We don't say anything when Brian Giles grounds out to third. Or when Josh Fogg strikes out. Or when a commercial comes on where a bunch of guys drinking beer get their dog to get them a six-pack.

Then there's a commercial for Just for Men. Jake puts his arm over the back of the couch and turns in my direction. Which makes me jump out of my seat, and means Mr. Furry practically gets dumped off the couch, which means she gives me a highly annoyed look and goes over and sits with Jake after all.

I consider going upstairs and reading *National Geographic for Kids* for the 185th time, but instead, I get up, go into the kitchen, and try to figure what to do. Which is when I see the ingredients for the orange meal sitting out on the counter, obviously for Jake's special good-luck-at-rehab final dinner, which, at this point is only 138 minutes away.

So I grab the Cheetos and go back into the den and start openly eating them.

Finally, in the top of the fifth, Pokey Reese hits this amazing double, which turns into an amazing triple on account of the other team's bad fielding, and for however long it takes for the whole thing to happen, I sort of forget about how I'm not speaking to Jake. Although, technically we don't exactly speak to each other, we just whoop the exact same whoop at the exact same time. Which totally annoys Mr. Furry, who jumps off the couch and waits for all the ruckus to end so she can go back to being petted.

After things quiet down, she blinks, looks at Jake, then at me. Then she jumps up on my lap.

I look sideways at Jake, who looks surprisingly bummed out. At which point, I decide that we can continue this stupid custody war over Mr. Furry for the next 133 minutes. Or that I can offer him some Cheetos.

Which I do, not actually saying anything, just holding the bag out in his direction. Which, if you think about it, is the kind of thing you can do without making it seem like you're actually doing anything, at least not anything important or meaningful.

Jake doesn't notice.

I clear my throat.

He won't look my way.

Finally, I shake the bag to get his attention.

He looks over at me like he could care less.

Which means that I act like I could care less that he could care less. I put the bag back in my lap.

We sit there not moving until the bottom of the ninth, although I have no idea what's actually happening in the game. All I do is count down the hits, strikes, and outs until it's practically over, and when it is—when the sportscasters are making the kind of time-killing jokes they make when everybody knows the game is over even if it isn't technically over—I pick up the bag of Cheetos and dump the whole thing over Jake's head.

The next thing I know, Jake has hold of my shirt and I'm falling backward off the couch. Then we're on the floor, kicking and grabbing at each other like crazy and taking wild swipes that don't connect. Jake swings at my jaw. I duck and he misses. I grab for his arm and end up ripping his shirt.

Then, at some point, I'm on top. I lock my fist,

cock my elbow just the way Jake taught me, and punch him, square in the stomach. He doubles up with a groan.

I sit back on my heels a second, then all of sudden, Jake rears up and throws me over on my back. He's just about to land a punch to my jaw, when I roll away, grabbing his shirt at the same time, and throw him back on the rug. His head hits the edge of the coffee table and something falls on the floor with a bang.

Fights have a rhythm, a definite-but-not-spoken feeling that both people get that tells them when it's over.

It was over.

We look at each other, both of us breathing hard. There's a line of blood over Jake's left eye and a bare, surprisingly white patch of skin that shows through where I ripped the neck of his shirt. My hand feels numb from where I banged it on the coffee table, but that's about it.

We sit there on the rug in the middle of a bunch of pulverized Cheetos, panting, both knowing I won.

Jake goes through a bunch of bogus moves like tucking his shirt in and fixing his hair, to make it seem like it's no big deal, which makes me feel sort of embarrassed but also sort of proud.

He dabs at the cut on his eyebrow. "Blood," he says, actually sounding sort of satisfied.

I don't know what to say.

"I'm gonna pay you back, you know," Jake says.

Normally, when one person says "I'm gonna pay you back," it means that he's pretty much admitting that he lost but that he's going to punch, headlock, or pinch the other one as soon as he gets the chance. Which means the other one pretty much always says "Oh, yeah?" Which means he's also going to try to punch, headlock, or pinch the other one before he gets the chance.

"Oh, yeah?" I say.

He reaches behind him and picks up the lampshade, which is the thing that got knocked on the floor while we were wrestling. "You know, for the Stargell."

"Oh."

Jake taps at the lampshade, trying to undent it. "Even though I know that's not enough to make it up to you."

I want to tell him I'm done collecting cards. Which is true.

But the other part, about it not being enough, is also true.

"You'll come back?" I don't plan on saying this. It just comes out.

"Of course," Jake says. "Why wouldn't I?"

I shrug. All I know is that when people in this family start coming home at 1:16, they end up coming home later and later until eventually they stop coming home at all.

"You promise?"

He nods.

"And you won't, you know, be like that again?"

He shrugs.

He needs to promise.

Which he doesn't do.

I look away and fold my arms across my chest.

We sit there for a long time, not saying anything. Then I look over at him. He's pulling on a thread from where I ripped his shirt.

"I'll try," he says. "That's all I can say."

And something heavy and tight inside my chest opens up. Just a little.

Which is when Mr. Furry wanders in and starts nosing around in the Cheeto debris. Which gives me an idea.

"We can blame it on Mr. Furry," I say.

Jake doesn't get it, at first.

"The lamp. We can say she knocked it over."

I look over at Mr. Furry, who's shaking her head

and licking her whiskers like mad, trying to get rid of Cheeto dust. She can take the blame for the lamp, I decide. She owes me.

Jake stands up and gets the Dustbuster. I straighten up the furniture and try to put the lamp back together while Jake cleans up the Cheetos. With both of us working, we're done in time to watch the post-game interview with Pokey Reese. Which at least gives us something to talk about. Not something important or meaningful. Just something regular. Which feels surprisingly good. Because somehow talking about regular stuff actually feels like it *is* important and meaningful.

When our mom comes down and sees me and Jake sitting together on the couch like regular, she doesn't say anything. Which is good, since the last thing you want when you're doing something like acting regular with someone you haven't been regular with, is to have someone else point it out. She also seems to fall for the Mr. Furry-as-lamp-wrecker story.

She looks at her watch. I look at mine. Which says there's only 52 minutes left till dinner. Which all of a sudden makes me feel surprisingly bad. I look over at

Jake, who is now looking scared and confused and a bunch of other things that I can't quite figure out.

"I'm going to start dinner," my mom says. "We're having the orange meal." She says this in a fake cheery voice but her eyes are full of tears.

I know what to do without even thinking. "Oh, Mom," I say. "I've got some bad news."

She looks sort of worried. "What?" she says. "What is it?"

She and Jake both look at me.

"Mr. Furry ate all the Cheetos."

It isn't the most hysterical joke anybody ever made, but Jake laughs, and then Mom laughs, and I think maybe Martha MacDowell's right. Maybe I am funny.

Our mom makes us walk over to the Mini Mart and buy more Cheetos with our own money, which, if you think about it, is letting us off easy since she probably knows that Mr. Furry is just about as guilty of breaking the lamp as she is of eating the Cheetos.

"You're pretty good at that," Jake says on the way to the Mini Mart.

"Good at what?"

"Lying to Mom."

I think maybe he means it as a compliment, but it

doesn't exactly feel like one. I don't *lie* to Mom. I just say things to keep her from getting upset.

"Don't take this the wrong way," Jake says. "Okay?"

I shrug.

"The way you always made up stuff so that Mom wouldn't know what was going on; the way you cleaned up after me and my friends and went around spraying the house with that orange stuff; it made me mad, you know."

I didn't know.

"At first I sort of liked it," he says. "It was like you were on my side. But after a while, I felt like you thought you were better than me."

"I was just trying to help," I say.

"Really?" Jake looks like he doesn't totally believe me.

I look away, over at the Mini Mart video camera, which shows Jake with his ripped shirt and his cut eyebrow looking like a juvenile delinquent. And which shows me walking just far enough ahead so it doesn't look like we're together.

I wasn't just trying to help. I wanted to be the hero. I liked being the good one, the one who took care of everything, who cleaned up the messes and made sure our mom didn't go back to smoking and crying and watching Lifetime TV all day. Jake was the bad one.

For not missing the old house and the old days, and for turning into someone who called you Dillweed in front of his friends, and for almost getting us both killed by a bread truck.

Which I thought gave me the right to feel like killing him, and wishing he would go to jail, and even sometimes wishing he wasn't even my brother.

Which, no matter what, he is.

I grab a bag of Cheetos off the shelf and rip it open, even though it's technically illegal since we haven't paid for it yet, and even though I'm being recorded on the Mini Mart's video camera. I hand the bag to Jake.

"Go ahead," I say.

"What?"

"Dump it on me."

He just looks at me.

"Go ahead," I say. "I deserve it."

Jake looks like he's considering the idea. "Nah," he says. He starts walking toward the cash register, then turns around. "Besides, it would be a waste of Cheetos."

* * *

The big-haired woman at the checkout doesn't say anything about how the bag of Cheetos are already opened, and Jake and I don't say anything, either. We just pay for it and leave. And we don't say anything to each other on the way home, or even when we get home and sit back down in front of the TV again while our mom makes the orange meal.

Until Jake gets up during a commercial and turns the Implosion family photo facedown.

"*You're* the one who does that?" I say.

"Does what?"

"The thing with the picture."

"Yup."

I wait for a while. "Why?" I said.

Jake doesn't answer.

"You've been doing it ever since we moved here, haven't you?"

Jake shrugs in a way that can mean yes or no, but which definitely means yes.

And I think then that I understand, really understand, what Mr. D meant about not caring about things in case they disappear on you.

I get up and turn the picture faceup.

Jake doesn't move. He doesn't call me a dillweed, or

punch, headlock, or pinch me. Or get up and turn the picture over again. He doesn't do anything. Which actually makes me feel surprisingly great. Because sometimes a person just knows when nothing is actually something.

Acknowledgments

My first thank-you goes to Alessandra Balzer, my editor at Hyperion, who was both gentle and strong in her stewardship of this book and whose skill and professionalism are exceeded only by her warmth. I also had the good fortune to work with Stephen Roxburgh at the book's inception, and with David Levithan, who gave patient and wise counsel as a friend and colleague. I also want to extend particular thanks to my agent, Nina Collins, and to Angus Killick and the crack marketing staff at Hyperion.

I am also grateful to The Writers Room, The Virginia Center for the Creative Arts, and the New York Foundation on the Arts for their support.

I owe a special debt of gratitude to the friends who sustained me during the period in which the book was written—Bridget Taylor, Hallie Cohen, Annie and Steve Murphy, Cathy Bailey, Meg Drislane, Beth Robinson, Bill Ecenbarger, Paul Rankin, and Joan Gillis. I'm also grateful for the support of my colleagues at the Writers Room—especially A.M. Homes, Mark Millhone, and Mark Belair—and to Shelley Messing, Sue Novack, and my Tuesday-night sisters.

It is my family to whom I am most indebted—to my parents and sisters who put up with my early attempts at writing—and, most of all, to Brandon, Kelly, Meaghan, Matt, and Paul, who teach me daily about the power of love and forgiveness.